CARNIV L

MURDER TIMES TWO

RON LOVELL

Two Thomas Martindale Novellas

INNOCENT

Ron Lovell

Penman
PRODUCTIONS

P.O. Box 400, Gleneden Beach, Oregon 97388
martindalemysteries.com
penmanproductions.com

Books in the Thomas Martindale Series

Murder at Yaquina Head
Dead Whales Tell No Tales
Lights, Camera, MURDER!
Murder Below Zero
Searching for Murder
Descent into Madness
Yaquina White
Murder in E-flat Major
Murder in the Steens

DEDICATION

*To my longtime friend Bob Webster (1934–2013)
for his many years of friendship.*

SPECIAL THANKS

To Dick Clark for the idea and editorial help on *Carnival*.

To Nick Sharma for the idea and editorial help on *Innocent*.

To Liz Kingslien, my designer, and Mardelle Kunz, my editor, for turning words on a manuscript page into something readers would enjoy looking at and reading.

CARNIVAL

"There was something about clowns that was worse than zombies. Or maybe something that was the same. When you see a zombie you want to laugh at first. When you see a clown, most people get a little nervous. There's the pallor and the cakey mortician-style makeup, the shuffling and the untidy hair. Clowns were probably malicious. . . . Zombies weren't much of anything. They didn't carry musical instruments and they didn't care whether you laughed at them. You always knew what zombies wanted."

—Kelly Link, *The Living Dead*

TOM

THE RINGING OF THE PHONE WOKE ME from a sound sleep on my first morning home in several weeks. In my early morning stupor, I reached for my cell phone. No response. The ringing continued.

It was my land line, which few people use anymore. Old-fashioned guy that I am, I like clarity in my calls whenever I can get it. There's no "Can you hear me now?" befuddlement in my conversations on the land line.

"Hello." I cleared my throat. "Hello."

"Tom? It's a voice from your past."

A pause by both of us.

"Maxine?"

"You got it. How are you?"

Maxine March had once been the love of my life. Five years ago I had repeatedly made a fool of myself in my pursuit of her. That had never happened to me before and I had trouble processing my behavior. Confirmed bachelor, studious professor, experienced journalist, book writer—in short, someone who tries to be detached and above the fray, both from affairs of the heart and in my writing. In my world, bad things happen—not to me, but to other people—and I write about them.

When our breakup came, Maxine flaunted her affairs—with an older man, a noted photographer who was old enough to be her father, and a U.S. Army special ops guy who had been my close friend. This happened after I had been thrown in jail on suspicion of killing her. Lorenzo Madrid, a superior attorney who is now one of my best friends, got me off by proving that she was not dead. A year later, I saved her from a murderous drug gang, but I was relieved when we parted and hadn't really thought of her much in the years since.

A bit confusing? That is putting it mildly.

"I'm surprised to hear from you," I said coldly.

"You sound sleepy," she said. "Did I wake you?"

"That's okay. It was time to get up anyway. Are you in New York still?"

"Still in New York."

"Still shooting?"

"Still shooting." Maxine had inherited the older man's photography studio when he died, along with his archive of prints and his customers. She was a gifted photographer in her own right.

"God, that can't be easy these days."

"I'm lucky to have good contacts, here and overseas."

I felt like asking how many of her contacts shared her bed but that would be rude. My guiding principle after someone betrays me is to cut them off and not see them again. In the years since we parted—after a dramatic shouting match at a lighthouse on the Oregon coast—she had vanished, not only from my life but from my memory. Like that great line from Dr. Zhivago that says of the character Lara that she "vanished without a trace . . . , forgotten as a nameless number on a list that afterwards got mislaid."

"So, to what do I owe the honor of your call?" I asked her.

"You sound angry, Tom. Surely you can't still be . . ."

"Maxine, I don't want to get into it. Our time together happened a long time ago. I've moved on, and I presume you have too."

There was a long silence before either of us said anything.

"Let me cut to the chase," I said. "What do you want?"

"I had forgotten how rude you can be," she said.

"Okay, Maxine. I am being rude. You called me for a reason, and I'm trying to find out why. That's all."

"I'm trying to decide if I should let you help me," she said finally.

More silence by both of us, and then she starting laughing. After a few seconds, I joined in. "Okay, okay. I'll tone down the bitterness a bit. I don't want to overplay my wounded pride persona."

"That's the Tom I know and care about."

I let that remark pass and waited.

"I'm on assignment for *Smithsonian*, the magazine, to document American carnivals; they're calling it 'Carnival Faces.' It'll be featured in the magazine, and I may get a show out of it later."

"Congratulations. That's great news. All of your years of hard work have paid off. When do you start?"

"I've already done two-thirds of the work. I'm focusing on three old-time carnivals—in the East, the Midwest, and the Pacific Northwest. The first two are done. The reason for my call is that the outfit I want to photograph—Mammoth Shows—is coming to your part of the coast next month. Ever heard of Taft-by-the-Bay? Is that near you?"

I hesitated, then replied, "Yeah, it's a tiny town near Lincoln City about thirty minutes north of me. I know it well. What can I do to help you? I'm fresh out of contacts in the carnival world. Academia is a circus, but not a carnival."

She ignored my sarcasm about my sometime profession. "I need to make my plans, but the owner won't respond to my letters or return my phone calls. I'm about to fly to Ecuador for another assignment, and I'd like to know that this carnival thing is all set before I leave."

"I'm impressed. Foreign assignment to Ecuador. Doing it for a magazine?"

"Don't I wish," she said. "It's for something called the International Business Consortium, based in London. They support small businesses in Third World countries. Strictly PR stuff. Not sure of the exact details yet. The pay is good and, besides, I'm not in a position to turn anything down, especially when it involves work overseas."

"That should be very interesting." I thought for a moment, but I really didn't want to do anything that would put Maxine back into my life, even for a short while. "Let me see what I can do to help you."

"Wonderful. Thanks so much. The carnival is being sponsored by the local chamber of commerce. You know everyone so I figured you'd have a contact there."

"I'll try my best. How can I reach you?"

"I'm leaving New York at the end of the week." She gave me her cell phone number and her email address.

"I'll check around and get back to you as soon as I can."

"Tom, thank you. I hope we can be fr . . ."

Hanging up on people is the epitome of rudeness, but I did it anyway. I stared at the receiver for a few seconds before putting it down and walking into the bathroom.

MAXINE

THE FLIGHT FROM NEW YORK TO QUITO WAS LONG, but Maxine's decision to splurge and pay for business class made it bearable. She doubted the expense account for this assignment would allow the extra luxury, but she needed to arrive as rested as possible. Riding in the tourist section for twelve hours would be exhausting. The extra money spent was worth it.

Soon after the LAN-Ecuador plane took off from Kennedy airport, handsome Chilean stewards were offering her drinks and snacks and newspapers and magazines. Once the plane had gained its designated altitude, her steward, Juan Carlo, offered wine or a mixed drink. The first of three meals came next. The console in front of her contained at least fifty movies, all available at the press of a button. No U.S. airline that she had flown on had ever been this good, even in first class. In Maxine's view, the money-grubbing airlines in the states cared nothing about passengers, only their stockholders and financial bottom lines.

As was her normal ritual, she pulled two of her cameras out of her carrying case to make sure they were working properly.

The seat next to her was empty so she was able to put the case and some lenses on it as she wiped them off.

After dinner, she put the cameras away and pushed the seat back a bit, donning the sleep mask Juan Carlo had given her. She awoke an hour later to find someone sitting next to her: a man in his thirties, blond, slender, and good looking.

"Sorry if I woke you," he said, extending his hand. "Seth Barlow."

"Maxine March. Hello. No, I didn't hear you. I guess I was more tired than I thought. I really conked out."

"I had to change seats to get away from that woman with the kid. She kept asking me to hold him or help her feed him. Next thing I'd probably have to burp him. I don't have kids, and I don't want to have kids, not even for just a few hours."

Maxine yawned. "I know what you mean. It's been career all the way for me."

"You're a photographer," he said. "I noticed you had your cameras out earlier. Looked like you're getting ready to take more than tourist shots of Incan ruins and Galapagos tortoises."

"Yeah, you got me. I make my living taking photos."

Barlow signaled for the steward.

Juan Carlo was at their seats instantly. "*Si señor?*"

"I'd like vodka on the rocks," Barlow said. "What will you have, Maxine?"

"Not sure if it's too early or too late for something strong," she said. "Oh, what the hell. Give me scotch and soda."

As Juan Carlo walked away, Barlow said, "The drinks will relax us and maybe put us to sleep."

Maxine liked Barlow's easy manner.

"So, what do you do, Seth?"

9

"I'm with the American embassy in Quito. Agricultural attaché or some dumb shit title like that. I hang around the office and go out in the countryside to tell farmers a better way to do what they've been doing successfully for hundreds of years."

"You don't sound too happy about your work," she said, smiling and taking a sip of the drink Juan Carlo had just handed her.

"Well, it's a nice pay check, and I like the tax advantages of living overseas. I get housing provided and a car too, but enough about my boring life. What kind of assignment will you be doing down here? Ecuador is pretty much off the international radar, unless you know something I don't."

"I'm not doing a news story. I've been hired to take photos of various small businesses here. My client is the International Business Consortium based in London. The photos will be used for publicity stuff—brochures, annual reports, press kits. The usual PR stuff. They've got a new initiative starting in South America, and Ecuador is the first country on the list."

"Sounds pretty mundane for you," he said.

"Why do you say that?"

"You strike me as someone who likes adventure. I'll bet you would rather be covering a war or a coup. Something exciting."

Maxine shrugged her shoulders and laughed. "You got me pegged right. But these are tough times for journalism and freelance photographers most of all. We've got to take what we can get. I do my share of magazine and newspaper work, but these days I don't feel I can turn down anything."

"What have you got in mind to take photos of?" he asked.

She pulled out a notebook. "Let's see—tuna fishing in Manta and Panama hat making in Montecristi. Do you know either of those places?"

"Yeah, I've been to both cities. Nice people, but it's pretty dry and dusty in Monte. Manta is on the ocean so it's prettier."

"I was really surprised to learn that Panama hats are not made in Panama but in Ecuador, many of them in Montecristi," she said. "Did you know that?"

Barlow ignored her question and quickly changed the subject. "Say, why don't we spend some time together in Quito before you disappear into the sticks? I've got a nice place near the embassy, and you're welcome to stay with me."

"Look, Seth, I'm very flattered and you are quite a hunk if I may say, but I try to tend to business when I'm on these trips. I can be easily distracted."

At that point, he grabbed her and began kissing her passionately.

"Whoa," she said, pulling away. "Let's take it easy here. Any other time, I'd like to spend my days lolling around with you, believe me. I'm no prude, but I've got to . . ."

"Yeah, yeah, yeah. Work on those damn photos. You could take some shots of me, dressed or undressed. I don't give a fuck."

"Maybe you need some coffee, buddy."

"You think I made a pass at you because I'm drunk? Not at all, *señora*. You can't say you didn't like our little kiss."

"Is everything all right here?" asked Juan Carlo, who Maxine was very glad to see.

"Fuck off, Juanito!" shouted Barlow. "The lady and I are having a discussion that does not involve you. Go off and count the liquor bottles or change that baby's diapers. He's been crying for hours. Better still, stuff that diaper in his mouth!"

"*Señor* Barlow, I must ask you to lower your voice. Others are sleeping," Juan Carlo said, then turned to Maxine. "Do you wish to change seats?"

Maxine was torn. Seth Barlow was easy to look at and easy to talk to, but she didn't like where this conversation was going, and he had an animal ferocity about him that scared her.

"Seth, maybe it would be good for you to go back to your seat," she said. "I need to use that seat to sort through my gear to get ready for tomorrow. I've only got a few days in Ecuador, and I've got to make every minute count."

Seth shrugged and did not make the fuss Maxine feared he would. "Okay, I give up. Suit yourself. But you don't know what you're missing. Here, take my card in case you get lonely in Quito."

He handed Maxine a card, then stepped over her and into the aisle. As he did, he made sure the bulge in his pants brushed her hand. He glared at Juan Carlo. "See ya!"

TOM

AFTER BREAKFAST, I READ THE MORNING PAPER and tidied up my house—anything to delay trying to figure out who to call to help Maxine get permission to take her photos. If I felt that way, why did I agree to try to help her? Beats me, but here I was, phoning an old friend.

"Captain Dan's Pirate Pastry. Dan speaking."

"Danny Morgan, I presume. This is your old friend, Tom Martindale."

"Did you say Wink Martindale, the TV star of yesteryear?" Dan can be a very funny guy, although this wasn't one of his greatest lines.

"I think Wink died a long time ago. I'm Tom, his son."

"Oh yes, didn't you used to be somebody?"

"And I still am, in the minds of my fans."

"In the immortal words of Groucho Marx, 'On a hot day like today, I could use a big fan.' Seriously, how are you, Tom? We haven't seen much of you lately."

Dan Morgan and his wife, Kathy, started their pirate-themed bakery six years ago, after both retired from careers in banking.

13

Despite the downturn in the economy at the end of the Bush years, they had prospered. Now they sell all kind of coffees and pastries made by Kathy, based on her mother's and grandmother's recipes. Dan is the front man, entertaining the customers—and occasionally scaring the children—with his pirate talk and bad puns while wearing the requisite tricornered pirate hat. He shouts "It's a great day to be a pirate" or "How arrrrrrrreeee ya?" as he waits on his amused customers.

Dan Morgan is also the part-time mayor of the tiny tourist town of Taft-by-the-Bay, a wide spot along Highway 101 and 53rd Street that caters to tourists with its many hotels and restaurants, many of them on or near the Pacific Ocean.

"I've been doing a lot of traveling to promote my book," I said. "I haven't been in because I haven't been around."

"We need to remedy that, matey," he said. "You need to drop by."

"How about in an hour? I've got something to talk to you about."

"Sounds ominous."

"Not really, but you need to put on your mayor's hat."

"Sounds portentous or pretentious, I'm not sure which," he said.

"Whatever you say. The grammar police are not on duty this morning."

Both Dan and Kathy were helping customers when I walked in the back door, so I sat at a table and waited for them to be free. In a few minutes, Dan joined me at the table. Kathy walked over and hugged me, then said she had to get back to her baking. "I've got several wedding cakes to do before tomorrow."

"I understand," I said, then turned to Dan. "Can we go back to your office?"

"Wow, this must be big," he replied, laughing.

We walked to the small office in the rear of the shop, and he motioned me toward a chair opposite his small desk. "Kind of tight quarters, but we can have some privacy. Close the door. So, what's up? Why all the secrecy?"

"You know about the carnival that's coming to town?"

"Oh yeah. I had to co-sign the permits for the city," he said.

I told him about Maxine's assignment to take photos of the carnival people and the failure of the managers to respond to her messages. "Can you tell me who to see to get the approval for her?"

Dan reached into a drawer of his desk and pulled out a folder.

"The chamber of commerce and the city are co-sponsors. Says here that the manager of the carnival is a guy named Hank Carson. Not sure if he owns the outfit, but he runs everything. He's who I have been dealing with. He's actually coming to town this afternoon to look over the site. I told him I'd meet him there. Why don't you join us?"

"Great. That would be perfect. I can find out if he got Maxine's requests and if he'll agree to let her hang around and take photos. Where's the carnival going to be set up?"

"Right down 53rd near the ocean by the turnaround. There's a large plot of land the city owns where we want to build a park if we ever get the money. I'll meet you there in, say, two hours."

We shook hands and I left the shop, waving to Kathy who was waiting on some customers.

"You need to try my marionberry scones when you come in again," she shouted.

"I will do that, but what about my diet?"

MAXINE

MAXINE SPENT HER FIRST DAY IN QUITO doing touristy things—the cathedral, the palace, the historical museum—to get used to the time change and the altitude. She loved what she saw. The historic central city was untouched by the blight of ugly skyscrapers. In fact, according to a guidebook she read on the plane, Quito had been declared a World Heritage Site by UNESCO in the 1970s for having the best preserved and least altered historic city center in Latin America.

While walking around the old city taking photos, she realized that the faces of people in the street were all that she had hoped for as photo subjects: faces with character, mainly Indian features and dark brown skin, with a smattering of lighter-skinned people of Spanish descent.

Later that afternoon, when she walked into the lobby of her hotel, a familiar figure got up from a chair and walked toward her.

"Hello, Seth. How did you find me?"

"I've got my sources," he said, smiling. "Actually, it wasn't that hard. I figured you'd be staying in the best hotel, and this is it. Come sit with me for a minute." He led her to a sofa and sat in a chair next to her. "So, how was your first day?"

"It was absolutely wonderful. I have never seen a city with so many interesting looking people. I used every camera and every lens I have." She gestured toward the two cameras she had placed on the seat beside her and the camera bag on the floor at her feet.

"You must have a lot invested in all that gear," he said.

"You bet. It's the way I make a living. I try to keep up with the latest stuff, but it's hard because something new is coming out all the time." Maxine looked him over. "So, how are you? How are things in the agricultural attaché business?"

"Same old, same old," he said. "But I want to talk about you and the fact that you are going to go out with me for dinner tonight. You need to see Quito after dark—it's a very different city from Quito in the daytime."

"I'm pretty tired—jet lag and all." A list of excuses ran through her mind, although part of her wanted to say yes. "I've got to leave here day after tomorrow, and I need to get ready for my assignment. I've got a conference call in the morning with the people I'm working for in London, and I need to figure out what to ask them. I took this assignment in a hurry and didn't ask many questions. I don't even know who my guide is. Plus, a girl has to get her beauty sleep."

"Whoa, whoa, I get it!" he said, feigning disappointment and pretending to pout. "You sure know how to hurt a guy. Come on, it's just a simple dinner. I know a place near here that serves the best ceviche in all of Ecuador. I'll have you back by ten."

Maxine sighed. "Okay. I'll do it, but I need to be back early. Let me go up to my room to drop off my cameras and change. I'll be back in fifteen minutes."

"Need any help with your zippers?" he said with a smirk.

She got up and gathered her gear. "I'm a button girl," she said over her shoulder. "No zippers."

Dinner was as good as Seth said it would be. They had the ceviche, followed by a course of rice and beef, then dessert and coffee to finish the meal.

"That was fabulous," she said. "I am stuffed to the proverbial gills. Thanks for bringing me here. I appreciate your hospitality."

"Have another glass of wine," he said. "I think it's from Chile. Very smooth and gentle, like me."

Maxine ignored that remark and changed the subject. "So I guess I'll be going into a whole other region when I go to Manta and Montecristi."

"That's right. You're in what they call La Sierra here, the highlands of the Andes Mountains. We're at almost 10,000 feet here. If you're a bit short of breath, that's why. You'll be going to La Costa. There's also La Amazonia, the rain forest, and the Galapagos Islands, some six hundred miles off shore where those giant tortoises are."

Maxine pushed back her chair and started to stand up. She shook her head. "Wow. I seem to have a buzz on. I didn't drink that much. . . ." Then it hit her. "You bastard. Did you? . . . "

As unobtrusively as he could, Seth Barlow helped Maxine toward the door. He put his arm around her as if they were lovers heading home after a good dinner. He waved away all offers of help and got her into a cab. The address he gave the driver, however, was not her hotel but his house.

TOM

Dᴀɴ Mᴏʀɢᴀɴ ᴡᴀs ᴀʟʀᴇᴀᴅʏ ᴀᴛ ᴛʜᴇ sɪᴛᴇ where the carnival would be set up when I arrived. He got out of his car and walked toward me.

"Top of the mornin' to ya," he said in his pirate voice. "How arrrrrr ya?"

"Are you into your Johnny Depp persona even out of the shop?" I laughed.

"Sorry. I do get carried away." He had taken off his tricornered hat and put on a baseball cap with the words *Pirates have more fun* on the front. "Hank Carson said he'd meet me at two, and it's later than that already. I hope he gets here soon—I've got to make some deliveries this afternoon."

Just then, a very old Lincoln limousine pulled up to the curb, half blocking the street. A man wearing a priest's garb got out from the driver's seat, walked to the rear door, and opened it.

The man who got out from the back looked like he belonged in a carnival. He was short and fat with features that seemed slightly askew: a nose that had been broken more than once,

21

ears shaped like cauliflowers, and a mouth that did not quite hide the fact that he was missing several teeth. He bounded out of the car with such speed that he seemed at first to be on the verge of toppling over and rolling away from us until the priest caught him and pushed him upright.

"Mighty fine, mighty fine, Father Eddie," the short man said. "Thank you, thank you." He looked at Dan and me for the first time and squinted as if he could not quite bring us into focus. His attentive companion quickly slipped a pair of glasses onto his face. "Mighty fine, mighty fine, Father Eddie." His voice had the cadence of the 1930s movie actor W.C. Fields.

Dan stepped forward. "Mr. Carson, welcome to Taft-by-the-Bay. My name is Dan Morgan and I'm the mayor. This is my friend Tom Martindale."

I stepped forward to shake Carson's gnarled hand, but he did not raise his.

"From the look of this burg," Carson said over his shoulder to the priest, "you've got your work cut out for you."

Both of them then started laughing loudly, the kind of out-of-control display that leaves people coughing and their eyes watering. Dan and I did not join in the merriment, however.

"Excuse me, dear sirs," Carson said after a few more minutes of guffaws and choking. "Just a little jest to lighten the mood. Actually, this is a lovely spot, a lovely spot. Our little band of merrymakers will be enchanted to perform here for the assembled throng."

"I'm not sure how big a throng is," said Morgan. "We are only a small town, but your show will probably draw people from the surrounding areas."

"Not to worry, my lad, not to worry," Carson said, shaking his head. "You will be surprised at the magic we can make. Am I right, good padre?"

The priest stepped forward. "Right as rain, which I gather the Oregon coast is noted for."

"But hopefully the gods will prevail, and we will be spared any such calamity while we're here," said Carson. "Now, let's see what we've got here."

The priest took Carson's arm and led him toward a large open space.

"Lead on, Sir Pirate. I am but a poor buccaneer, ready to follow you to the ends of the Earth," said Carson, causing them to start laughing again.

"This empty lot will probably be big enough," said Morgan.

We walked to the back of the lot, along the perimeter, and then back to where we had begun.

"How large is this space?" Carson asked.

"Almost four acres," said Morgan. "It's the largest open area in town."

"More than enough space, don't you agree, Father Eddie?"

"Yes, sir. You can have the Midway over there and set up the rides along the other side."

"And don't forget we need plenty of room for our star attraction, the Zipper. We cannot neglect that stupendous product of genius."

Dan and I looked at each other and at the same time said, "What's a zipper?"

Carson and the priest smiled.

"Good padre, pray tell these esteemed gentlemen about our star attraction."

The priest cleared his throat. "Well, good sirs, the Zipper is something to behold. It has an oblong frame, called the boom, which rotates like a Ferris wheel. There are cars suspended evenly along the perimeter of the boom, which are moved by pulleys around the sides. The cars hold two people and are built of metal mesh to protect those kind souls who dare to enter them. The cars flip around quickly when the whole apparatus turns, and since they are in the odd-looking shape of apostrophes, they appear to be the interlocking teeth of a zipper."

The priest had been using his arms to explain the shape of the contraption, and he now dropped them to his sides. "I guess I sound like a promotional brochure," he said. "It's just that I . . . I love this ride, and I know it well."

"Well spoken, my learned friend," said Carson, reaching up to pat Eddie on the back. "Very well done."

Both looked at us for approval.

"Sounds scary," I said.

"Is it safe?" asked Morgan. "I mean, it sounds like a death trap, if you don't mind me being a bit blunt."

"Bluntness can be a virtue, my pirate friend, but sounding alarms where none are warranted is tempting the devil to do his evil work."

"Tempting Lucifer himself," said the priest.

"I was only playing the devil's advocate," replied Morgan.

"DO NOT SPEAK OF THE DEVIL IN MY PRESENCE," shouted Carson. "I have been under his evil spell more than once during my years on this Earth." There was a sudden change in his demeanor as he continued. "If you persist on using his name in my presence, I will have to cancel our appearances in your fair city."

Father Eddie pulled out a binder from a briefcase he had been carrying for Carson. "Here are some statistics from the National Carnival Association and, as you can see, the Zipper is the safest ride of all listed here. More people get injured on merry-go-rounds than on the Zipper." Eddie thrust the report in Morgan's face but moved it up and down quickly as his finger pointed at several lines, then whisked the pages away before Dan could really focus on the print.

"Okay, okay," Morgan said, backing away with both hands up. "I believe you. You certainly know your business better than I ever will. I presume you've got insurance?"

"Up the proverbial kazoo, my pirate friend," said Carson. "And the city would be covered for its outdoor events. Right?"

"Yes, it is. I checked on that yesterday, and it's in this agreement I need you to sign now. I sent you a copy last week, and I imagine you have read it," Morgan said, handing a paper to Carson.

"Indeed I did, indeed I did," Carson replied. He looked at the priest who pulled out a pen from the briefcase and handed it to him. Carson put the document on the hood of his car and signed all copies with a flourish. "You realize how lucky you are to get us on such short notice," he said. "We had another town bail out for . . . um . . . reasons I won't get into now."

The priest nodded as if to reaffirm what Carson had told us.

"We will begin moving in tomorrow," Carson said, looking around the property. "We are a mobile organization—everything travels by truck, trailer, and motor home. We will set up our rides in front and park our trailers and motor homes at the rear. I see there's a chain-link fence along both sides and the back. That's good. Can we have some kind of fencing across the front?"

"I spoke to our city works director, and he said he could put a low fence across here, like the kind used to keep sand from covering streets in a storm," said Morgan.

"Then I guess we are done here," said Carson, as he turned and started toward the car. The priest walked quickly ahead to open the door.

"One more thing, Mr. Carson," I said.

Both he and the priest turned to face me.

"Mr. Martin, was it?" said Carson. "I wondered if you were mute."

"Martindale, but Tom is fine. I came with Dan to meet you and ask a favor."

"And that would be what?" A smirk crossed Carson's face. He narrowed his eyes. "Okay, I'm listening."

"A close friend of mine, Maxine March, is a photographer, a very good photographer. She has won awards and gets her work published in only the most well-known and prestigious magazines. She wrote to you, last month I think, about wanting to photograph the people who work in your carnival. She's already taken photos in carnivals in the East and Midwest, and she wants to include a carnival out here in the Pacific Northwest."

Carson snapped his fingers and the priest pulled a sheet of paper from the briefcase. Carson adjusted his glasses and glanced at the letter.

"Says here that your friend is from New York City."

"Yes, she works there but travels a lot, nationally and internationally."

"Maxine. That's an old-fashioned name. Don't hear it much anymore. When I hear it I think of the Andrews Sisters, a big singing act in the 1940s. One of them was named Maxine."

"I've heard of them," I said.

"You have?" said Dan. "You ARE old!"

"Maxine told me once that her grandfather insisted on that name for her because of how much the singers meant to him during World War II." Turning to Carson, I said, "So obviously, you have her letter and are considering her request?"

"Yes, yes. I guess the letter got lost in the shuffle."

I doubted that, given the priest's ability to keep his boss organized.

"This young woman is impatient, I take it?" commented Carson.

"No more than anyone else needing to make plans. Maxine is a freelance photographer so she can't turn down any assignment that comes her way. This one is from the *Smithsonian* magazine, and she can't afford to disappoint the editors there. She needs to know if she has to find another carnival."

"I wonder why she picked us?" said Carson. "We are not the biggest show around."

"But we are by far the best, boss," said the priest.

"That was probably the reason, no doubt," I said. "Also, she wants a carnival from this region. The Northwest is where you play, right?"

"Okay, I'll tell you what I'm gonna do. I'll let your Maxine come here and take photos of us, but she has to agree that I have the final word as to what she photographs. Will she agree to that?"

"I don't know. I'll have to ask her. She is a photojournalist, and no journalist likes to be censored in any . . ."

"I AM NOT A CENSOR," shouted Carson, his face turning red. "I HAVE NOTHING TO HIDE!"

Given his anger, I was sure that just the reverse was true. Did he cut corners from the safety standpoint? Did he not pay taxes on all of the money he brought in? I had read that carnivals were an all-cash business, and that operators even paid their bills in cash.

"I'm sure you do not, and I wasn't saying you did. I will contact her tonight and ask her. This is a feature story, not a news story, so I don't think you have anything to worry about. There may not even be any story, only the photos. You see, it's the faces she wants—you and Father Eddie, for example, and your other cast members and the people who attend your shows. The working title is 'Carnival Faces.' That kind of says it all."

Carson thought for a moment. "Okay, I'll let her into our magical world, and I'll give her as much access as I can. We've got to keep a few secrets, though, like any proper business. We aren't a bunch of rubes, Mr. Martin. We are professional entertainers."

"I'm sure you are, and I did not mean to imply otherwise."

As he started to walk away, Carson turned back and said, "I need to tell you, though, that I plan to hold you personally responsible for her conduct."

Carson gave me a look that left no doubt in my mind that by granting me this favor I would somehow be indebted to him. As usual, helping a friend seemed to be leading me into something I might regret.

MAXINE

MAXINE WAS FULLY DRESSED when she woke up at nine the following morning. A slight breeze ruffled the curtains hanging from the open glass doors leading to what appeared to be a balcony. She sat up and swung her legs around and stood up. Her shoes were placed so she could easily step into them. Her purse and shawl were lying on a chair across the room.

The last thing she remembered was Seth Barlow leading her out of the bar. She had been unable to resist and feared the worst as she passed out.

Then she noticed a piece of paper on a table by the bed.

Off to do my job. Make yourself at home. You may need lots of coffee. You were pretty drunk last night. Nothing happened, in case you can't remember. You are in my guest room, not my bedroom, in case you didn't notice. Stay as long as you want.

Hope to see you around. Seth

Maxine believed him, why she did not know. Her head hurt but her body did not feel violated, although she did not know

29

precisely how that might feel. She got up and walked around the apartment to make sure she was alone. It was tastefully furnished and quite large. There were few personal items around, however, as if Barlow didn't spend much time actually living in it. She walked back into the guest room and through to the bathroom where she took off her clothes. The hot water of the shower felt good on her skin and revived her. She dressed quickly and left the apartment. Outside, she stepped onto the street of a very upscale neighborhood and hailed a cab to get back to the hotel.

As she walked into the lobby, a desk clerk called to her.

"*Señora* March, you have a message and also a gift."

Maxine walked to the desk, and the clerk handed her a slip of paper and a bouquet of flowers.

"From an admirer, no doubt," he beamed and bowed slightly. "I have taken the liberty of putting them in a vase to keep them fresh in your room. Do you want me to have someone carry them up for you?"

"No, no. Thank you. I think I can manage." She reached into her purse and pulled out a five-dollar bill. "*Muchas gracias,* Sebastian."

"My pleasure, *Señora* March."

Back in her room, Maxine pulled out the business card she had noticed tucked along the side of her wallet. She saw that it was one of Barlow's, but with no phone number or even title, just his name.

She walked to the desk in her room and picked up the phone. "Would you please connect me to the American embassy."

"*Uno momento, señora.*"

"American embassy. How may I direct your call?"

"Yes, good morning. I am trying to reach one of your employees. I believe he is the agricultural attaché."

"Name please, and I will connect you."

"Seth Barlow. I met him on the plane flying down. I am . . ."

"I am sorry, madam, but there is no listing for a Seth Barlow, either working here in the embassy or at one of our other locations."

"But he told me he worked . . ."

"I have given you all the information I can, madam."

TOM

BEFORE WE PARTED LATER IN THE DAY, Danny Morgan and I agreed that Hank Carson was one of the strangest people we had ever met.

"He goes way beyond me and the antics I sometimes use when I'm in my pirate garb and trying to sell treasure cookies to little children," Morgan said. "He is one weird gent. And what about Father Eddie? Yikes! I wouldn't take communion from him or even let him say grace at my table for Christmas dinner!"

"You having any second thoughts about giving the carnival a permit to set up here?" I asked.

"Naw. The public will love it, and we need to bring people here," he said. "You know how it is over here on the coast: you've gotta make your money in the summer to get you through the winter. We'll have help from the sheriff and the Oregon State Police to keep these carnies in line."

When I got home I did several Internet searches for Mammoth Shows and got a lot of information that I already knew. Carson owned the majority interest in the carnival but had two partners with names that sounded like they were small-town businessmen—Wally Larkin and Elmer D. Jones.

Because it was privately owned, there were no financial figures available. I did find a quote in the *Wall Street Journal* from Carson about the effects of the recession on his business. "We're holding our own," he told the reporter, "because carnivals offer a fairly cheap kind of family entertainment. We're not like Disneyland or one of those places where it costs a fortune to take your kids for a day of fun." The same article had a quote from a spokesman for Disneyland which touted that theme park's reduced rates for families.

I also found articles involving Mammoth's safety record. All involved problems with the ride Carson had been so proud of—the Zipper.

As far back as 1977, the Consumer Product Safety Commission had issued public warnings urging carnival-goers not to ride the Zipper after four deaths occurred when compartment doors opened in the middle of the ride and riders fell to their deaths. The spring-close latches had worn out and did not hold. Even after safety features were added, two teenage girls were ejected from their compartment when the door flew open because a safety latch had not been inserted when the door was closed. They survived but were badly injured. Newer models of the Zipper include an improved door lock. They have also made the compartments heavier and reduced the spinning, which decreased the pressure on the latches. Hopefully, Carson's was one of the newer models.

Despite more searches, I could not find any information on Carson himself or any of the performers. The website for Mammoth Shows was nothing more than a sales tool, with a calendar of appearance dates and the prices for the shows. So I decided to turn my attention to my next promotional trip, this one to Europe. Although my publisher took care of some of the arrangements and the cost, I liked to make the actual reservations myself.

But first, I had to contact Maxine. She had asked me to keep her updated on my quest for permission to take her photos. I had her cell phone number, but I didn't want to pay long distance charges, so I emailed her.

Maxine. Mammoth Shows will let you take your photos. The boss wants approval, which we can deal with later. Let me know your plans and if you need hotel reservations. Call me with any questions. See you soon, I think. Tom

MAXINE

Maxine had little time to ponder the strangeness of Seth Barlow. He was definitely not an agricultural attaché as he had said. Instead, he was probably in the CIA or even in a military intelligence unit. She would probably never see him again, something she regretted because he was very attractive. As was always the case with her, however, work came first. She had one more day of shooting in Quito before going to Manta and then into the interior.

However, the note she had been handed by the desk clerk offered another possibility. It was from Inez Santiago-Verde, a Spanish photographer she had met in Madrid the year before. They had hit it off and loved getting together to swap war stories about how they were better at their jobs than their male colleagues. Both had subsequently gone to South Africa to cover rioting in the gold mines there.

> *Saw your name on the hotel register. How grand.*
> *Meet me in the bar at six. Inez*

When Maxine got there, Inez was seated in a booth in the back corner of the bar, surrounded by men—young, old, rich, shabbily dressed. The men were laughing, and Maxine could tell that Inez was loving every minute of the attention. She was dressed like a fashion model in an expensive-looking suit, silk blouse, and pearls. Her black hair was pulled back from her face. Her dark eyes were hidden by over-sized dark glasses, which she wore despite the fact that it was night and the room was dimly lit.

"Oh, my dears," she chirped, "make way for my darling friend Maxine. We have known each other for simply ages, and we must talk now to catch up. Now shoo, shoo like good boys." She raised her well-manicured hand and motioned for them to leave. They all stood up and did just that, several pausing to kiss her hand.

"I'll be in Quito for a while," she said. "More than enough time to renew our friendships. Give my best to your wives." Then she laughed heartily.

"Have a drink, my love," she said, as she motioned for Maxine to sit next to her in the booth. The waiter appeared instantly and Inez ordered. "Now, what are you doing in Quito, my darling? You must tell me all before I burst with curiosity."

During dinner, Maxine brought Inez up to date on her life. She mentioned the carnival assignment in the states and her reason for being in Ecuador.

"That man you mentioned who is helping you, that Tom person . . ."

Maxine had barely touched her drink but ordered a new one with no ice. "Yes, what about him?"

"Wasn't he the one you broke up with after that terrible fight?"

"Yes, that's him. I hated to call him for help, but I guess I'll do anything for an assignment. I swallowed my pride and called."

"And what happened? Surely he greeted you with open arms?" Inez laughed loudly, as if she could guess Maxine's answer.

"Hardly. He would barely talk to me at first, but then I warmed him up and he agreed to try to use his contacts to get permission for me to take my photos." The waiter placed the new drink on the table, and Maxine continued. "He's a pro and knows how journalism works, especially photojournalism and the sad state it's in. He knows that every assignment is precious."

"Is he a working journalist now?" asked Inez.

"No, he's a journalism professor in Oregon and the author of several best-selling books," said Maxine.

"Impressive. Are you afraid that you two will become entwined again when you see each other—running madly toward each other across the burning sand with the waves crashing against the shore?"

It was Maxine's turn to laugh at Inez and her overly romantic imagination. "I don't think so. I do hope we can become friends again, though. I liked him a lot and learned a lot from him. I was his student back in the day, you see."

"Ah ha!" Inez said, laughing again. "The plot begins to get very thick, indeed!"

Maxine spent her last day in Quito taking photos around town. When she returned to the hotel late that afternoon, Inez was waiting for her at the front desk.

"I hoped I could catch up with you, Maxine. I wondered if you would like to go with me on a small adventure." In her dramatic way of speaking, Inez held up a hand with the thumb and first finger almost touching. "Very tiny, but maybe fun and only slightly dangerous."

"I'm almost hooked, Inez. What's it about?"

"Well, my darling," she said, motioning for Maxine to sit next to her on a nearby couch, "there is a rumor going around that the Ecuadorian government is about to auction off large tracts of land in its Amazonian rain forest to several Chinese companies. At least, that is what my sources tell me. The area is home to a number of native tribes who, my sources also tell me, do not want their lifestyle and their environment despoiled by oil drilling."

She lowered her voice to a whisper. "This fact is not widely known yet. I want to fly there to see if I can get some photos of the area and, if I am lucky, actually see some Chinese faces hanging around."

"If this is only a rumor, I gather that the Ecuadorians want to keep this quiet?" asked Maxine.

"Yes, at least for now," Inez replied. "The president of Ecuador does not like the United States all that much and would love to sign this agreement to spite the big, bad U.S. of A."

"So, how will we get there?"

Inez smiled broadly. "So, you will accompany me? *Muy bien.* I love your spirit of adventure, Maxine. I have booked us on something called 'the Amazon Adventure' which flies over the area and stops briefly along the Napo River. There we will get out and stretch our legs while they refuel. We'll take it from there and then see what we find."

"When do we leave?"

"Early tomorrow morning. A car will pick us up here at the hotel at five o'clock and take us to the airport."

"I'll be ready," said Maxine. "I can contact my bosses in London and postpone my appointments to later in the week."

"Don't worry, cherie," said Inez, "I don't expect us to be gone very long. Think of it as a little vacation."

TOM

WHETHER IT WAS BECAUSE OF Hank Carson's bizarre behavior or the spotty safety record of the Zipper or the lack of background information on the carnival itself, I decided I needed more information. I guess my reportorial instincts had kicked in. Besides, I was waiting for my European book tour to start, so I had some time.

Several years ago, I served on the national board of a journalism society for two years and, in the process, met a number of reporters and editors from newspapers all over the country. A few broadcasters too. One of them was Pat Loomis, an investigative reporter with the *Cleveland Plain-Dealer*. We had kept in touch over the years, and I decided to call him at his home to see if he knew anything about Mammoth Shows. I noticed on their website that the carnival had played there the year before.

"Pat. Hi. It's Tom Martindale."

"You son of a gun. How are ya doin'?"

"Good. You?"

"Great. I'm about to hang up my reporter's tools and head for your world. I'm going to teach journalism at Ohio State in the fall."

"Good for you, Pat. You'll like it, except maybe the politics. And the students will love you. That's the best part of college teaching—the students you get to know and, if you're lucky, help launch on their careers."

"How about you?" he asked. "Last time we talked you were about to finish your book. From what I read, that project has turned out well for you, I mean, a bestseller. Come on. You've got to be reeling in a lot of bucks."

"Yeah, I guess. I didn't do it for the money, but the royalty checks are nice to get."

"I'll just bet they are."

"Pat, I don't want to take up too much of your time, but I called for a reason. Have you ever heard of a company called Mammoth Shows? It's an outfit that puts on carnivals all over the country."

"Shit, man, you bet I've heard of them. I did several stories on them last year when they set up in a small town near Cleveland."

"I guess you got to know the boss, Hank Carson?"

"Know is not the word I'd use. More like tolerate. That bastard. He left town in the dead of night without paying his bills. Lots of people lost money on him and his outfit. Bunch of crooks. Not only did they con the visitors to the Midway, they also didn't pay the local workers and suppliers of stuff like food and soft drinks."

"How'd he get away with it?"

"Pure guile, I guess. You know carnivals are a totally cash business. They rake in the money for admission and rides but don't take credit cards. So you've got thousands of dollars of income, a lot of it not declared on tax returns. I think Carson just uses as little of the cash as is necessary to pay off local cops. I'm pretty sure that happened here with at least one sheriff."

"Makes sense," I said.

"What brought Mammoth Shows and the disreputable Mr. Carson onto your radar out there?" asked Pat.

"The show is setting up in a small town near me, and I talked to Carson about letting a photographer friend of mine roam the carnival for an assignment she's doing for *Smithsonian*."

"Good luck to her. I hope that she doesn't meet with foul play!"

"That bad?"

"Might be. There were some reported rapes of local girls by some of Carson's men."

I couldn't imagine Maxine ever getting in a position where she'd be raped. "Doubt that Maxine will have to worry," I said. "She's worked all over the world and knows how to take care of herself. I'll warn her, but I know her well enough to believe that she won't let anything stand in the way of completing her assignment. You know how you journalists are, Pat."

"Yeah, we're a pretty determined bunch when it comes to completing assignments, especially on a juicy story. Listen, I've got to run to my boy's Little League game. How about I fax you some stuff I dug up but didn't use in my story. I'll send the story too. The bosses here got cold feet about including some of this stuff, so my story was not exactly of award-winning caliber."

"Great, Pat. Thanks very much." I gave him my fax number. "Good to catch up with you, and good luck in your teaching career. You will love it."

I fussed around my desk for fifteen minutes or so, and then the light on my fax machine came on and it started spitting out the pages from Pat.

BACKGROUND ON MAMMOTH SHOWS

Hank Carson—this manager is a short and fat man with an extra round mid-section. His girth makes him wobble when he walks and, at times, he seems like he will tip over. But he is very confident, especially in his ability to make money. So he waddles around the carnival with assurance.

Hank is in his mid-50s but looks older after too many late nights and too much fried food. Lots of in-your-face arguing has made his voice raspy. His hair is white and thinning.

Hank grew up in the carnival business in Nevada. His mother and father owned a carnival show that traveled the West year round. They began in the Southwest in the winter and gradually moved north as the weather got warmer. Because of this nomadic existence, Hank did not attend school regularly. He learned math by counting greasy dollar bills taken in at the shows. He learned to read by perusing carnival ride maintenance manuals.

Hank can pull back on his aggressive action when he has to—like with local leaders in communities where he wants the show to play. He can paint a friendly smile on his face, like any carnival clown, to get what he wants.

Hank travels in an expensive BMW SUV with the driver's seat extended back so he can wedge himself behind the steering wheel. But his prize possession is his traveling office. He modified a forty-foot trailer into a combination bank—for counting the daily take—and luxurious office, complete with conference room.

Like everything else in his life, Hank's desk is large and solid. By raising it off the floor on a six-inch platform, he always looks down on the people who come to see him. This helps him maintain his not-so-subtle air of intimidation.

While Hank may not pay attention at all times, an assistant records every word. But the "assistant" is not like your normal secretary—it is a colorful parrot named Mr. Rambo. It is all white with yellow on its head, beady black eyes, and a beak so sharp it can open tin cans. Mr. Rambo has the unusual ability to hear conversations and then repeat back key phrases, which both charms and unnerves visitors. This is especially true when Hank asks Mr. Rambo a question, as in: "What do you think we should do, Mr. Rambo?"

Often the parrot replies, "Hank does not think that is a fair deal."

Mr. Rambo is part companion and part night watchman. He always stays in the trailer after hours like a sentry to cry his alarm if anyone comes into Hank's office without permission.

Father Eddie—this old friend of Hank's is a Catholic priest in disgrace. He had been thrown out of the church for molesting two teenage boys ten years before. Hank met him while attending an "unofficial" service over which the priest presided. The priest's ritual reminded Hank of some of the carnival's best performers, like the fire-eater or the sword-swallower. What amazed him the most was that the priest collected money without even asking for it. In the carnival, you really had to work for it.

When they met, Hank and Eddie hit it off immediately, so Hank invited him to travel with the carnival. Eddie had always been fascinated with the energy and variety of carnivals. He once told Hank that he always wanted to be a clown.

"Be my guest," said Hank. "Anytime."

MAXINE

TWO COUPLES WERE STANDING alongside the small plane at a remote part of the Quito airport when the taxi pulled up the next morning. The pilot/tour guide stepped forward and helped Inez and Maxine with their bags. Both traveled light, needing to bring a lot of camera gear rather than very many clothes. ("All you need in the jungle is a change of underwear, mosquito repellent, and Chanel #5," Inez had told Maxine the night before.) Since Maxine had checked out of her hotel, Humberto stashed the rest of her luggage in the back of the plane.

"Humberto Diaz, at your service, *señoras.*" The pilot was young and very good looking with light brown skin, bright blue eyes, and a small mustache that set off his brilliantly white teeth nicely.

"You have a face that is *muy magnifico,*" said Inez. "I must photograph you immediately." She raised her camera and started snapping away. Humberto looked embarrassed and slightly helpless.

"I think we're holding up the show here," Maxine whispered to Inez.

"Oh, sorry."

She walked over to the others and introduced herself. A Japanese couple bowed and mumbled their names. Maxine walked behind Inez and shook hands with them. Next in line was a typical-looking American couple.

"Agnes and Buddy Jackson, from Mobile, Alabama."

They were dressed in shorts, brightly colored T-shirts, and down vests. He had on a canvas hat with a wide brim and she a Panama hat.

"I like your hat," said Maxine. "Did you get it here in Ecuador?"

"No, honey, I ordered it over the Internet, through our travel club in Mobile," said Agnes.

"Got us a nice discount too and free shipping," Buddy chimed in.

"I don't want to break up your conversation," said Humberto, "but we need to get going so we can reach the Napo River in time for lunch and a little bit of sightseeing."

The six passengers climbed into the plane and belted up. In a few minutes, Humberto had them airborne. They flew out of the populated area of Quito and were soon over heavily forested terrain, so dense that it was difficult to see the ground in most places.

Humberto started his tour guiding as soon as he had leveled off. "Ecuador, officially called the Republic of Ecuador, which literally translates as Republic of the Equator, is a representative democratic republic in South America. It is bordered by Colombia on the north, Peru on the east and south, and the Pacific Ocean to the west. It also includes the Galapagos Islands out in the Pacific, about six hundred miles west of the mainland. That area is known for its giant tortoises.

"The main spoken language is Spanish but two other languages of official use in native communities are Quichua and Shuar. Ecuador became independent from Spain in 1830. Before the Spanish came, Ecuador was part of the Inca Empire of Peru, starting in 1463."

Humberto turned in his seat. "Am I going too fast for you? We have much to cover today and there is also a lot of material in the booklets that were placed on your seats before you boarded this aircraft. Okay to continue?"

The six of them nodded, although it seemed to Maxine that the Japanese couple was looking very perplexed.

"Ecuador has three main geographic regions, plus the islands in the Pacific that I mentioned previously. There is La Costa, the low-lying land along the ocean; La Sierra, the high-altitude belt running north-south through the center of the country and the Andes mountain range; and La Amazonia, the rain forest area which comprises just under half of the total surface area but holds less than five percent of the population."

By this time, both the Japanese couple and the Alabamians were dozing. Inez was shooting image after image out the window. Only Maxine was listening to the guide, who continued talking, unaware that he had lost most of his audience.

In another hour or so, the plane began to descend, flying lower and lower in a slow circle to give the passengers a wide view of the jungle that began at the river's edge. They made a smooth landing on the beach, which was as long as any small airport in the United States. Humberto turned the plane around and taxied to where a small building stood. He powered down the engines and turned to the passenger area.

"Welcome to La Amazonia," he said, smiling. "Let me assist you as you climb down." He jumped down out of the plane and reached for a small wooden box tucked inside a small compartment in the door.

As the six passengers got out, a woman came out of the building carrying a tray of glasses and fruit. "Welcome to La Amazonia," she said, smiling. "We are very glad to have you here."

Humberto put his arm around her and kissed her on the forehead. "My sister, Anamaria."

"Thank God," muttered Inez. "I was afraid she was his wife. He is too cute to be saddled with a wife." She began taking pictures of the couple.

"You are free to walk around but do not go too far," he said. "We will leave here in one hour and then fly to our next stop, a native village to the south, where we will have lunch."

Maxine and Inez headed straight for the jungle, leaving the others along the water. As they walked away, Humberto's radio crackled to life, with a man's voice shouting something unintelligible. Then Humberto started waving his arms at them and shouting, but Maxine and Inez had already disappeared into the dense jungle.

The ever-resourceful Inez pulled out a small hatchet and started hacking a path for them. "If my sources were not lying to me, there should be an exploratory well site about a mile ahead of us," she shouted over her shoulder.

"A mile?" groaned Maxine, out of breath. "God."

In ten minutes, Inez stopped and sat down on a log. "We can rest for a few minutes. I don't think Humberto will leave without us. Bad for business."

"So, what's the real story about our little adventure?" asked Maxine.

"The Ecuadorian government owes a lot of money to the Chinese government—$7 billion," said Inez. "The Chinese are always looking for new sources of oil to fuel their growing economy. It is not news that the drilling has begun and that Ecuador is even building a large oil refinery. The native groups are opposed to this and have protested loudly but without success. Last year, the Inter-American Court on Human Rights issued a ruling that prohibited oil development in the Sarayaku, a tropical rain forest that begins near where we are. You can't get there except by plane or canoe. The court was trying to preserve the area's rich cultural heritage and biodiversity."

"Let me guess," said Maxine. "You have heard that the Ecuadorian government and the Chinese are going to do it anyway."

"Precisely," said Inez. "And I want to take back the photographic proof of this for all the world to see. Let's move on."

The two got to their feet and pressed on. In another ten minutes, they noticed an open space ahead of them. When they got to the edge of the jungle, they saw another river with wide sandy banks on both sides.

"Look over there," Inez shouted. "That's it!"

Maxine looked to the left and saw several trucks and a Land Rover parked next to a tall metal structure that straddled a hole in the ground. Both photographers began to snap away. Maxine aimed her long lens at the vehicles, specifically at the door of one of them, which looked to her to have Chinese lettering on it. As she shifted positions, the sun's rays caught the glass on her lens and cast a reflection toward the men she now saw standing at the hole. As she continued to take photos, one man turned with a shocked look on his face. Seth Barlow shaded his eyes and reached for his rifle.

Maxine and Inez saw his movement and ran back into the jungle. They leaped over downed trees and dodged thorny bushes as they raced back to the plane. With lungs nearly bursting, they covered the ground in twenty minutes.

Humberto was pacing back and forth, a gun in his hand and his sister at his side, looking worried. The others were already on board.

"Where have you been, *señoras?* I did not know what to do. We need to get going to keep to our schedule."

"Bring Anamaria with us, Humberto," shouted Maxine. "Bad men are after us. I'll explain later."

Humberto grabbed his sister's hand, and the four of them boarded the plane. He started the engines and taxied to the end of the beach. As he was readying for takeoff, one of the trucks they had seen before drove out onto the beach.

As the plane ascended, Maxine saw Barlow standing in the back of the truck. Although he fired his gun repeatedly, the bullets missed the plane, which headed south toward the burning midday sun.

TOM

MY NOSINESS WAS WHAT HAD MADE ME a fairly good reporter. In fact, I always loved journalism because as a reporter you can get people to tell you stuff before anyone else has heard about it. That same trait had gotten me into a number of messes in recent years, even after the end of my formal reporting career. Time after time I got into a lot of trouble—with both the law and some bad guys—because I asked too many questions and put myself in danger, usually to help friends.

Against my better judgment, I was probably going to do something similar to help Maxine. Her request involved only getting permission to take photos at the carnival. I had done that fairly easily. After meeting Hank Carson and the good Padre Eddie, however, I felt the need to find out more about the carnival and how it operated. I hadn't met two shadier characters in a whole career of meeting shady characters, and as angry as I had been with Maxine, I still didn't want to send her into anything that would be dangerous.

I looked up the travel schedule of Mammoth Shows and decided to pay a visit to The Dalles, the town where the carnival was stopping for five days before coming to the coast.

The Dalles is eighty miles east of Portland on the Columbia River. It is a historic trading town with a main street that looks pretty much like it has for fifty years, with many older buildings nicely restored and still occupied by a variety of businesses. It is also the home of Klindt's, Oregon's oldest bookstore. I had a book signing there two years ago when *The Cocaine Trail* came out. The Dalles is also the site of a Google data center, giving the town a nifty mix of the new doing business with the old.

I decided not to contact anyone I knew in town but just drive to the carnival site in a park east of town to see what I could find out. I doubted that Carson would remember me, but I wore dark glasses and a baseball cap in case I ran into him.

I heard the calliope-like music before I saw the actual carnival Midway. The booths were lined up along a main aisle that broke off into two. The rides, most of them mounted on large trucks, were along these two arteries. A merry-go-round and Ferris wheel, along with bumper cars and other smaller rides, were placed here. At the far end, both branches of the pathway met. It was there that the infamous Zipper had been set up.

I heard screams before I reached this ride. Young men and women and a few brave parents with children appeared to be hanging on for dear life as the individual cars flipped around wildly at the same time as they moved around the main boom. I stood back a while to watch.

It took about two minutes for the whole contraption to make its cycle. People got into each car from a wooden platform. The ride moved forward and the cars started rocking immediately, even when things stopped so the next passengers could get into the next car.

The ride was full on this pleasant evening. At the time I stood watching, a line of about twenty people had formed, mostly young couples of high school age, full of enthusiasm despite the fact that several people immediately threw up when they stepped off the ride.

"God, I've never been so scared in my life!"

"I mean, like wow! What a thrill!"

"You mean, what a death trap! That thing's not fuckin' safe! I'm tellin' my dad!"

"Whatever."

The kids moved off to buy some popcorn and cotton candy at a nearby stand. I noticed that as soon as the ride emptied and more people were getting into the cars, two workmen who had been standing next to the ride quickly darted under the structure. With what looked like small metal detectors, they picked up coins that had obviously dropped out of the pants pockets and purses of the previous riders.

These men were joined by Eddie, who held out a plastic bag into which the men quickly placed their loot. One man held up a watch and the other a ring. As soon as they were finished, Eddie twisted the top of the bag and walked off. I followed at a distance.

He walked to a large motor home with an OFFICE sign and went in. I walked nonchalantly to the rear with the hope that I could look inside. Luckily, the vehicle was parked next to some tall bushes that might offer some cover from the lights and the people walking by.

The motor home had a rear door with a small wooden step pushed up to it. I picked it up and moved it in front of a small window at the back, stepped onto it, and peered in.

Father Eddie was standing in front of a large desk that was raised on a platform—just as Pat's information had indicated. He placed the bag onto the desk and stepped back. Fat hands reached out, picked up the bag, and emptied the contents onto the surface.

I couldn't hear what was being said clearly enough to understand it. The man at the desk, presumably Hank Carson, reached down and placed a metal box on the desk. He opened it and put the money, watches, and rings in it and closed the lid. Then the hands began stacking $20 bills in neat piles and banding them. As I had read, carnivals are a cash business, indeed.

I leaned over to make sure it was Carson. As I did so, I reached for the window frame to steady myself, and it squeaked as I pulled on it. That attracted the attention of Mr. Rambo, the parrot, which I now saw on its perch next to the desk.

It turned its head and beady eyes toward the window and saw me. It began squawking loudly, "INTRUDER ALERT, INTRUDER ALERT! ALL HANDS ON DECK! ALL HANDS ON DECK!"

I ducked behind a large boulder and then saw Father Eddie rush out the door and around to the side where I had been standing seconds before. He shrugged his shoulders and walked back to the front. As I crept away from the carnival, everything was quiet except for the mechanical droning of the Zipper and the occasional screams of the unfortunate occupants of that dangerous ride.

MAXINE

WHILE THE OTHER PASSENGERS CHATTERED about the incident at the air strip, Humberto asked Maxine and Inez to comfort his sister, who could not quit shaking. "She is only a country girl and not used to the violence we live with daily in the big cities," he whispered.

Maxine put her arm around the young woman and let her sob into her shoulder. "It's okay. We're going to be safe. Your brother is a good pilot, and he is also very brave."

Humberto motioned for Inez to sit in the copilot's seat after the plane had reached its cruising altitude. Maxine could not hear what they were saying, but she was sure it involved what had happened back in the jungle. As they flew over mile after mile of dense jungle, she wondered if they could survive a crash or a forced landing—in case the men with Seth Barlow had the means to pursue them in the air.

After ten minutes or so, Inez emerged from the cockpit and sat down next to Maxine and Anamaria, who was now asleep. "Humberto thinks we broke up some kind of meeting between the Chinese oil guys and the American," she whispered in Maxine's ear.

"I know that man," Maxine said quietly.

"You do? How is that possible?"

"It's a long story. I met him on the plane and later at dinner he drugged my drink and took me home and . . . nothing happened, but I don't trust him."

Inez gave her an understanding look.

"The main point," Maxine said, changing the subject, "is that I think Barlow is CIA. But why did he shoot at us?"

Inez sighed and moved closer to Maxine. "The reason he shot at us, I presume, is because he did not want anyone to know that he is meeting with the Chinese—or that the U.S. government is meeting with the Chinese. In my world, that is news."

"You're probably right," said Maxine, "but how can you prove it well enough to go into print?"

"I've got him nailed in some shots with my long lens," Inez said. "We only need to speculate that he is CIA. He looks American, after all. I've got an exclusive. European papers eat up this kind of thing—the CIA with their hands in the proverbial cookie jar. I don't have to have the positive truth of what I print, I just run a correction later, if necessary. That way, I keep my exclusive and get some money."

Maxine was skeptical, but this was Inez's show so she decided to stay out of it.

"And with your identification of him, that's all I need," Inez continued. "Some speculative headlines and, voila, we've hit pay dirt with a big story that may, as you say in America, have 'legs.' Many publications all around the world will want to run this story, I'm certain of that."

"How does Humberto know so much about this kind of thing?"

"That was precisely my question to him. His father was in the military and so was he," Inez replied. "I gather the family has money and is well connected."

"Are we in danger?"

"He thinks we should not return to our hotels."

"That's okay with me since I checked out before we left, and I have everything with me. I planned to go on to Manta and Montecristi when we returned; however, I don't think I want to stay in Ecuador any longer."

"Neither do I. I'm known here and always attract attention wherever I go. I'm on TV a lot, you see."

"What's going to happen to us?" said a rather weak voice from the rear of the plane. It was the lady from Alabama.

Inez got up and walked toward the other four passengers. "I am so sorry, my dears. We got so involved in comforting Anamaria that we forgot about you. Humberto said that what we saw was an isolated incident and probably a mistake. He said he has been taking tours to that part of Ecuador for years with never any trouble. As soon as we land and collect our luggage, he will arrange for transportation to your hotels."

The four of them nodded and seemed relieved. Maxine doubted they would have any trouble. They were obviously tourists, and everyone leaves tourists alone.

All conversation stopped for the rest of the flight. The small plane landed without incident, and Humberto taxied it to a small building away from the main terminal. There, two vans awaited them.

They all got off the plane and as Humberto unloaded the luggage, he directed the tourists to the first van. Humberto motioned for Maxine and Inez to stay behind, pointing to the second van. They all waved their farewells to the other people when their van drove away.

Humberto nodded to Inez and Maxine, and they headed for the second van. As they neared it, a car raced onto the runway and headed toward them. Bullets ricocheted off the ground and the van.

"RUN AS FAST AS YOU CAN!" shouted Humberto, pulling a gun.

Maxine and Inez dropped their larger bags and ran as fast as they could toward a large hangar. Several aircraft mechanics looked up from their work as the two ran inside. Humberto was right behind them, yelling to the men to hide. The women headed toward a stairway that led to a walkway extending around the inside of the entire building. They clambered up the steps and ducked into the first room they came to. It was a conference room of some kind, dominated by a large table. They sat down in two of the chairs.

"*Madre mia*," said Inez. "What a close call for us. Are you okay, cherie?"

Maxine looked down at herself. "Yeah, I'm fine. Just hard to get my breath." For the first time, she looked closely at Inez. "Your side. You're bleeding! We've got to get you to a doctor."

"No chance, my dear," she said, motioning toward the loud voices below. "I think they've found us."

Maxine lifted Inez's shirt and saw how bad the wound was. She pulled off her scarf and pushed it into the wound, but it did little to staunch the blood.

"Don't bother, my dear," said Inez weakly. "I've covered a lot of war zones so I know all about gunshot wounds. I want you to leave me and find somewhere to hide. Take my camera and make sure the film gets to London. My agent's name and number are inside the case. He'll make sure this gets into print and on the Internet. You can dictate the story to him. That way, we'll both have an exclusive. Not bad for a couple of middle-aged broads, right cherie? NOW GO!"

A shot rang out below, followed by a moan. Maxine knew Humberto was probably dead. She could hear footsteps on the walkway. She glanced around and took the only route to safety she could see.

Seth Barlow was the first man through the door. He ran to Inez and pulled her into an upright position.

"Glad to see my aim is still good," he said, sneering at her. "Where's your slutty friend? Did she tell you what nice games we played in my bed?"

Inez coughed and then spoke in a whisper. "All she mentioned was how pitiful you were. No *cojones* to speak of. And your penis? *Un poco.*"

She was laughing when Barlow snapped her neck, the blood from her wound pouring out onto her clothes and the floor.

Barlow walked around the room trying to see where Maxine might be hiding. By this time, four other men ran into the room, their guns drawn. Two looked Ecuadorian and two Chinese. A third Chinese man walked in and over to Barlow.

"I have never liked loose ends," he hissed. "You know what happens when I am displeased."

"I don't give a fuck how *displeased* you are. My neck is on the line here too. Don't you think I know that!"

The man walked up to Barlow and slapped his face. "You forget who is in charge here, Mr. Barlow! I am paying you a lot of money to do this work for me, so I make the rules and, as you Americans say, I call the shots! You would be wise to remember that." He looked down at Inez. The smell of Chanel #5 wafted up from her lifeless body. "An unfortunate turn of events for such a beautiful lady. Did you look for her camera? I know I saw it flash a number of times at the river."

"I couldn't find it," said Barlow, rubbing his face and glaring at the Chinese man.

"So that means the March woman has it. Had you not forced yourself on her, we might have been able to coax her to give it to you. Now, she is obviously on the run. It will be on your head if she isn't found and that camera retrieved." He snapped his fingers and his two men followed him out the door.

Barlow walked around the room again, checking for any sign of where Maxine had made her escape. The windows were painted shut and the ceiling seemed solid. He took a long pole and probed for loose tiles. A big heating vent was rusted shut. He shined a flashlight into the space and saw only the beady eyes of a rat looking back at him.

"We're done here!" he yelled at his men, and the three of them left the room.

Maxine was in shock and no wonder—Inez had died right before her eyes. She was so afraid that Barlow would find her that her teeth were chattering. It took all her self-control not to scream.

After at least a half-hour in the air-conditioning duct, when she could no longer hear any sounds from below, Maxine dared to move. The rats were all around but fortunately had not touched her. When she got to her feet, they scattered back into the duct.

"God, I hate rats," she whimpered and lowered herself to the floor. Then she walked toward Inez's body, her eyes filling with tears as she looked down at her friend. Inez's words echoed in her ears, "Be strong!" Her first instinct was to cry out for help, but no one nearby would be of any assistance. And maybe Barlow and the others were still around. She pulled out her cell phone and pressed a number she had not used for many months.

"Trans-Alaska Imports," said a familiar voice. "How may I assist you?"

"Paul, it's Maxine. I'm in real trouble, and I need your help badly."

PAUL

THE BUZZ OF HIS CELL PHONE startled Paul Bickford. The call was coming in on a number that he gave to very few people — only very close friends and two of the few relatives he had. He had also given it to Maxine March in a fit of passion after they had last made love the year before.

"I need you, baby," he had moaned at that time.

"So, how can we stay in touch?" she had asked, rolling over in the bed in her New York apartment. "I never know where you are. Hell, I doubt you even know where you are half the time."

"God, isn't that the truth. You know I love you but . . ."

"But your job comes first. I know, I know. I'm the same way. So a little roll in the hay from time to time is all I'm good for." She had faked a pout, then started smiling. "We are truly two peas in a pod. I enjoy our little trysts as much as you apparently do. Best to keep it that way."

"Even though our being together ended things with Tom?" he had said.

"He thought he wanted to be with me, but he really didn't. I was just convenient, like I am for you. But he got pretty needy and was so jealous of us. He showed his true colors—an uptight guy who can't commit himself to anyone. He's as addicted to work as we are."

"That shouting match you had at the lighthouse," Bickford had said. "That was the shouting match to end all shouting matches."

"I'm not sorry it happened," she had said. "All his histrionics, they were a big show. We never even had sex."

"Now that surprises me, the way he carried on," Bickford had said.

"I think we might be friends if we ever meet again," she had said.

The phone rang again, bringing him back to the present.

"Trans-Alaska Imports," he said. "How may I assist you?"

He never spoke his own name when he answered. Safer that way, even though anyone using this phone would be someone he could trust.

""Paul, it's Maxine. I'm in real trouble, and I need your help badly," she said, in a voice so low he could barely hear her.

"Maxine. God, it's been a . . ."

"A year. You know I wouldn't call you if I didn't really need you."

"Yeah, yeah, I know. I appreciate your . . ."

"Can you get me out of Ecuador?"

"Ecuador? God, what are you doing in Ecuador?"

"I'll explain later. I'm in danger."

"Where are you precisely?"

"I'm in an old hangar at the Quito airport on the side farthest away from the terminal." She started sobbing uncontrollably.

"Maxine. Take some deep breaths," he said. "Slow down and answer my questions. I can't help you if you don't calm down."

She collected herself and sighed.

"Are you hurt?" he asked.

"No, but a friend is dead. She's lying here next to me."

"And she is . . ."

"Inez Santiago-Verde, a Spanish photographer."

"I've seen her on TV," he said and then mumbled, "Makes it harder since another country is involved."

He waited so long to reply, Maxine thought the connection had been cut off. "Paul? Are you still there?"

"Are you in danger right now?" he replied.

"No, I think the bad guys have left this area. Not sure if they're still hanging around the airport, though. They already searched this building and didn't find me."

"I've brought your coordinates up on my GPS. Lie low and try to relax. Are you in shock?"

"I keep crying and wanting to scream, and my heart's beating pretty fast."

"Breathe deeply and try to calm down. Think of pleasant things—the Oregon coast or your favorite pet when you were little. Cover your friend with a coat or something so you don't have to keep seeing her. Someone will be there in an hour, two hours tops."

TOM

WHILE I WAITED TO HEAR FROM MAXINE, I decided to buy a new house. I had lived in the house in Newport for many years—first as a summer rental, more recently as an owner. It was small and the kitchen, bathroom, and carpeting were a bit out of date.

I had had a realtor friend looking for a more modern place for several months, and she called me about the same time I heard from Maxine this time.

The house was in Gleneden Beach, about twenty miles north of Newport. It had just been built so everything was new, and it was on a cul-de-sac, which would offer me the privacy and quiet I craved for my writing. Even though it was only 1,600 square feet, the space was spread over three floors so it looked bigger. There was a two-story living room, three bedrooms, and two baths. The kitchen, just off the living room, had newly installed granite countertops and a new range, dishwasher, and refrigerator.

Best of all was the spacious loft, which overlooked the living room. The minute I saw it, I knew that it would be my office. I could envision floor-to-ceiling bookshelves on every wall without a window and room for my writing table, a desk, and a computer area. It was, for me, the "clean, well-lighted space" Hemingway had spoken about.

With a lot of spare money in the bank—thanks to my best-selling drug book—I was able to pay cash. The seller snapped up my offer, even though it was $5,000 below his asking price. I sold my old house to a newly arrived scientist at the NOAA station in Newport, and she paid full price.

Today was moving day. I had packed all of my worldly goods over the past few weeks—including fifty boxes of books—and arranged for a mover.

It took three men six hours to move all of my stuff in, which included placing the furniture in each room so I would not have to move it later. Halfway through, I bought sandwiches and soft drinks for the men and ate lunch with them.

"Wow. You got a lot of books," said one young guy.

"Yeah, I guess I do."

"Yeah, like a fuckin' library."

"Yes, just like that."

"You read all of those?"

"Only half of them."

"No shit?"

"Yeah. I write books too."

"Fuckin' A! No kiddin'?"

"Yup."

"Got any more of those sandwiches?"

And so the lunch break went. The trio finished at about four o'clock and departed.

"Yo. Good luck with your new house, sir."

"Thanks. I appreciate that."

After they had driven away, I started unpacking. I had labeled the boxes carefully so the process of putting things away went fairly quickly. I finished the kitchen by six and the bedrooms by nine. I decided to save the books until the next day.

That night, the phone rang. I hoped it would be Maxine, telling me when she would arrive. I guess I wanted to get this business with her over with.

"Hello."

"Hi, Tom. It's Lorenzo."

"Lorenzo, my Latin heartthrob of an attorney. Always good to hear from you. How are things going?"

"All right, I guess."

"You sound down. Everything okay?"

"Yeah. Just bored with my life."

"That surprises me," I said. "You've always loved your work so much, helping the poor with their legal problems."

"Yeah, yeah, yeah," he said. "I'm still doing that."

"That's good."

"That's just it, Tom. I knock myself out for them and they wind up back in here, sometimes in even worse shape than when they came in the first time. Their problems are usually overwhelming, and they expect me to work miracles. I've been out of miracles for a long time. I can't do it anymore! And I'm lonely too."

"I'm no expert at either problem," I said. "I don't do much to help people anymore myself, since I quit teaching. The lonely part I can relate to, but my answer is to throw myself into my work. That hasn't worked for you, though, I guess."

"No, it only makes it worse," he sighed.

"Why don't you take a leave of absence and go on a trip or

teach at some college in a warm climate," I suggested. "Maybe you need a relationship with someone, which shouldn't be too difficult since women pass you their phone numbers every time we're out for dinner."

"You know I'm gay, Tom, so that won't work."

"Well, I've seen guys hit on you too," I said, laughing. "Go down to San Francisco and get married."

"Now you're making fun of me," he said.

"I didn't mean to. Sorry if you took it that way."

"No problem. I'm feeling kind of sensitive about everything right now. Well, I'll let you go," he said. "I just needed to vent a bit."

"How about I come over in a week or so and take you out to dinner?" I said. "Right now, I'm in the middle of helping an old friend you'll probably remember. Maxine March."

"I remember her well, but I also recall the big fight you two had at the coast," he said. "Your breakup sounded pretty final to me."

"It was that, but she's come back into my life, I hope briefly, for some help. It's a long story—I'll fill you in when we get together."

"It's a deal," he said, sounding a bit happier. "I'll look forward to seeing you soon."

Several years ago, I visited the home of the legendary author Jack London. It is now a California state park near the small town of Glen Ellen, not far from Napa Valley. He and his wife bought what he called the "Beauty Ranch" and lived in an old house on the property. The study where he wrote some of his most famous works is preserved as he left it when he died in 1924.

I toured the house on several occasions and was struck by the orderliness of that room. Many of his original manuscripts are there, carefully boxed and placed one per shelf, near his personal library of books. Many of the fifty books he wrote are on a special shelf in the living room.

The most striking area of the house for me was a small screened-in porch next to the study with only one piece of furniture: an iron cot over which was strung a clothesline with several old-fashioned wooden clothespins clamped on it. The great writer suffered a lifetime of insomnia, it seemed, so when ideas came to him in sleepless nights, he would jot them down on slips of paper kept by his bedside and hang them on the line to look over in the morning. Now THAT is dedication.

I would never go to that extreme, but I did like the idea of having all of my manuscripts and my reference files in one room. If nothing else, I gained inspiration from this prolific writer who was a journalist and a novelist and a chronicler of his own adventurous life. I picked up a file card onto which I had copied some of his words—I couldn't have said it better myself:

Don't write too much. Concentrate your sweat on one story, rather than dissipate it over a dozen. Don't loaf and invite inspiration; light out after it with a club, and if you don't get it you will nonetheless get something that looks remarkably like it. Set yourself a "stint" and see that you do that "stint" each day; you will have more words to your credit at the end of the year. Study the tricks of the writers who have arrived. They have mastered the tools with which you are cutting your teeth.

70

MAXINE

TRUE TO PAUL BICKFORD'S WORD, someone did show up, two hours later. Maxine had used an old tarp she found in a corner to cover Inez's body—her remains were beginning to smell and attract flies. Maxine's stomach was churning, even after she threw up several times. Her throat burned and she had the worst headache she ever had in her life.

She sat huddled in a corner of a small room next to the big space where they had taken refuge at first and alternately shook and sweated. This must be what shock is like, she thought.

At dusk, she heard a vehicle and hurried to the window at the back of the room. She had to rub the dirt away with her sleeve to see anything outside. An old truck had pulled up and a man got out. He looked like a farmer, from the straw hat on his head to the tattered jeans and jacket he was wearing. She doubted that Barlow would ever dress like this, nor did she think he would arrive in anything but a black SUV. She was tense, nonetheless, and held her breath as she waited with only a shard of glass as a weapon.

The footsteps resounded loudly on the bare floor. Clomp, clomp, clomp. Then silence as the man reached Inez's body. "Jesus Christ. You poor lady." The voice sounded young. Clomp, clomp, clomp. The man had reached her door. She tensed and held her breath.

"Miss March? Are you in there? It's okay. You're safe. I'm Sergeant Grogan, U.S. Army. Colonel Bickford sent me."

Hearing that, Maxine pulled the door open and practically fell into the startled soldier's arms. He put his arms around her and patted her on the back.

Maxine let him go and stepped back. "Sorry. It's just that . . . I'm so glad to see you. Thank you for coming."

"You are welcome, ma'am. We need to get you out of here pronto. And the . . . um . . . remains of your friend . . ."

"Inez Santiago-Verde, a Spanish journalist and wonderful friend."

"I'm sorry," he said. The sergeant was a good-looking African American with the fine features of a model. He was tall and slim and very muscular.

"Are you in Special Ops with Colonel Bickford?"

"Let's just say I've worked with the colonel for several years."

"Enough said. What do you want me to do?"

"We need to move Miss Santiago-Verde's body out to my truck. But first, please put on these clothes. They'll help you blend in better." He pulled some colorful clothes out of his backpack and handed them to her. "You can change in there," he said, pointing to the room where she had been hiding. "I'm going to carry the body down to my truck." Saying that, he picked up Inez's body, being careful that the tarp did not fall off, and left the building.

Maxine quickly changed into what she would later call peasant clothes—a colorful skirt and blouse and a black shawl. When she walked down the stairs and out into the narrow yard behind the building, Grogan was standing by the truck, holding the door open.

"You look like an Ecuadorian now," he said, smiling.

"But what about you? Are there . . ."

"Black people in Ecuador?" He smiled. "Oh, yes. The Spaniards brought them . . . us . . . here as slaves. I think my Spanish will convince anyone that I belong here."

They drove in silence for quite a while as Maxine thought about the predicament she was in and how she would get out of it. What would she do to finish her assignment? After all, her London-based employers had paid her expenses and were expecting the photos she had promised. Maybe she should go ahead and do her work. If she did not do that, how would she get out of the country?

She thought about all of these things, anything to get her mind off Inez.

"You know what, sergeant," she said, after more time had passed, "I think I'm going to finish the work I came here to do. I'm not going to let a bastard like Seth Barlow frighten me. And I'm going to avenge my friend Inez—she never left an assignment unfinished."

Grogan pulled the truck off to the side of the road. "That's not a good idea, ma'am. You aren't safe here. The colonel instructed me not to let you out of my sight until you were out of the country."

"Well, I won't object if you tag along with me. Ever been to Montecristi? It's inland from Manta. It's where they make

Panama hats. And you thought they were made in Panama. Me too!"

"I have my orders, ma'am."

"But I am not in the military, and I am not used to following orders. Can you call the colonel? Or let me call him. We are very old friends."

Grogan got out of the truck and walked into the brush, pulling out what Maxine took to be a satellite phone. She smiled and waved every time he looked in her direction. She could tell he was conflicted and had not wanted to make the call. Before long, he was talking and gesturing. Then he walked over to the truck and motioned for Maxine to step out.

"He wants to talk to you, ma'am."

She took the phone, which was so heavy she almost dropped it. "Paul, darling." She winked at the sergeant, who looked embarrassed.

"Maxine, I am not your darling," Bickford said. "You are ruining my reputation with my men who think I am as celibate as a monk."

"Oh, yes, I see what you mean," she said, smiling and winking at the sergeant, who turned away.

"Look, Maxine, I'm already going out on a limb here for you. The least you can do is to follow my orders."

"As I told the good sergeant, I am not in the military so I don't follow orders."

"How well I know that," sighed Bickford.

"So, what do we do here? Will you have the sergeant abandon me here in the jungle or will you . . ."

"Okay, okay, goddammit. As it happens, I can't get any transportation out of Ecuador for you until day after tomorrow. I

74

guess you will be as safe in this little town . . ."

"Montecristi, inland from Manta, a fishing port. Like the count, but spelled differently."

"Montecristi is small enough that Grogan can keep track of you and watch your back while you shoot your goddamn photos. I'll get you both out of there as soon as I can. Put the sergeant back on the line."

She handed the phone to Grogan.

"Yes, sir. I understand. She will never be far from me. Yes, sir, I will have eyes in the back of my head, for sure, sir. Goodbye."

They got back into the truck, and he drove it away.

"I knew he would see things my way," said Maxine, a note of triumph in her voice.

After a while, Grogan pulled off the road and switched on the GPS unit he had in his backpack to study it again. "We are here," he said, pointing to the screen, "but are nearing a crossroads up here. To the north is Quito. A van from the Spanish embassy is meeting us there to take possession of Miss Santiago-Verde's body. Then we turn west to Montecristi."

They reached the rendezvous point and saw a vehicle with diplomatic plates parked at the side of the road.

"There they are," Grogan said. "Just as the colonel planned."

"Is there anything he can't fix?" said Maxine, shaking her head. "No matter where you are, he knows someone — or someone who knows someone."

"Yes, ma'am. You got that right."

Grogan stopped the truck, got out, and walked over to the van. He talked briefly to the two men from the embassy and gestured toward Maxine. One of the men walked toward her. He was middle-aged but still nice looking. Wearing coveralls, he did not look like a diplomat.

"*Buenos días, Señora* March. My name is Pedro Sandoval, second secretary of the Spanish embassy. I have been authorized to offer you safe passage out of Ecuador early tomorrow morning. There will be no cost to you, I might add."

"*Gracias, Señor* Sandoval. I appreciate the offer, but I have business in Montecristi. Important business. I have discussed this with Colonel Bickford, and he agreed that Sergeant Grogan and I can go there and wait for him." This last was a lie, because she had no idea how Bickford planned to extract her.

"Well, I wanted to make the offer. Good day to you, *señora*, and safe travels to you." With that he signaled to the other man and they both walked to the back of the truck, presumably—because Maxine did not look—picked up Inez's body, and carried it to their van. Once they were inside, she could see through the open door that they put her in a body bag.

Maxine waved as the van drove away, tears running down her cheeks.

They did not reach Montecristi until after dark. Grogan drove up the dusty main road into the plaza, which was deserted except for a little boy of about eight or nine who seemed to be waiting for them. When Grogan saw him, he stopped the truck and got out. The boy ran up to him and hugged him around the legs.

"*Sergeanto, sergeanto.* You have returned to me."

"Hello, Tito. How is my favorite squirt?" Grogan took him around to Maxine's side of the truck. "Tito Morales, please meet *Señora* Maxine. She is a great lady from the United States."

"At your service, *señora*," said Tito, bowing gracefully. "I will help you like I always help the *sergeanto*. He is my favorite guy in the whole world."

"We need a hotel, my little pal. Can you recommend a nice one?" Grogan asked.

Tito smiled and looked at the two of them, first one and then the other. "For you two together, so you can smooch?"

Both Grogan and Maxine laughed loudly.

"No, no. Two rooms, one for each." Grogan put his hands together and then drew them apart slowly. "*Dos. Comprende?*"

"*Si, señor.* You need Black woman, not white one," said Tito.

"Maybe sometime but not tonight. Okay, my little pal?"

Tito smiled and pointed to a side street that connected to one edge of the plaza. "Cinco Sombreros," he said. "I take you there."

"No, Tito," said Grogan, handing several dollars to the boy. "You must go home for the night. You can meet us in the morning, and I will buy you breakfast. Okay? Go home now."

The boy shrugged his shoulders and hugged Grogan again. "*Mañana, mi amigo*," he said with a smile. "*Señora.*" He bowed to Maxine and walked away.

The desk clerk smiled knowingly as the two of them registered. "You want connecting rooms?"

"Not necessary, *señor*," said the sergeant. "We can even be on separate floors."

"A shame," said the clerk, sighing. "You require a late supper perhaps?"

Maxine and Grogan exchanged glances and both answered at once.

"Yes. Please."

★ ★ ★ ★ ★

"They probably won't let the kid into the hotel," said Grogan, when Maxine met him in the lobby the following morning. "They might have their own local kid for running errands and, anyway, they probably think a little peasant boy will drive away the tourists. How about if I put our stuff in the truck and then get something to go, and we sit in the plaza with him and eat?"

"Sounds perfect," she said.

At that moment, Tito came running along the street and up to Grogan, hugging him again.

"Good morning, little pal," Grogan said. "How is my favorite kid today?"

"*Muy bien, sergeanto*," he said, smiling. Then he bowed to Maxine. "*Señora*."

"Sit over there with the *señora*, Tito, and I will return with our food."

Maxine led Tito to a nearby bench and they sat down. Never one to miss the chance to take a good photo, Maxine lifted her camera and took some shots of the little boy. "You are very handsome, Tito," she said. "Are the girls after you?"

Tito blushed and shook his head. "I have no time for silly things like girls," he said. "I take care of *mi madre* and my baby brothers and sisters. I must work."

"That's very commendable, Tito."

The boy scratched his head. "Commend? . . ."

"It means you are very good," she said, bringing a big smile to the boy's face. "How about school? You do go to school, right? A smart guy like you should go to school."

"I go when I am not working."

"Does your padre work?"

"My father is in jail. He will be there a long time."

"Brothers who could help too?"

"One was killed by a gang, and the other one is in jail also." He looked sad. "There is only me." He jabbed a finger into his chest.

Maxine was near tears, so she changed the subject. "We are very happy that you are helping us today."

Tito smiled. "I would do anything for the *sergeanto*. He has helped me many times."

At that moment, Grogan returned carrying a large sack full of food. He brought out egg and bacon sandwiches and fried plantain and bananas, plus bottles of orange juice. He handed the food to Tito first and the boy began eating.

"Wait," said Grogan. "It is polite for us to serve the *señora* and wait until she lets us know when we can eat our food."

Maxine nodded her head and began eating. The other two joined in, and they all finished the food in ten minutes without saying a word.

"Really good, Grogan," said Maxine. "Thank you."

He smiled. "Glad to do it. Good Tito? Okay?"

"Very good, *sergeanto*. *Gracias*." The boy walked over to the sergeant and hugged him.

"Tito and I have worked together for a year or so. Right, Tito?"

The boy nodded.

Grogan looked around and spoke quietly. "The United States had a small base here in the nineties, to help the government stop the drug cartels from operating in Colombia. I was attached to that operation and spent time in the country when we shut it down last year. I did some travelling, and that's how I

79

met my young friend here." He reached over and patted Tito on the head. The boy smiled broadly. "He always helps me when I'm in Montecristi."

Then he said to Tito, "Would you go over there and buy us some bottles of water?" He handed the boy some money and watched as Tito walked away.

"The truth is, I'd love to adopt him and take him to the states with me. He's very bright and won't have much of a chance here. He's got a big family—single mother, father and a brother in jail, plus lots of younger brothers and sisters."

"He told me a little bit about that," Maxine said.

"I made some inquiries last trip, and it would be just about impossible to adopt him. There's so much red tape, and I doubt his mother would let him go, since he brings in most of the money. It makes me very sad."

Tito came running back and handed the two of them bottles of water.

"What do you say we start our day, partner?" said Grogan. "You will be our guide."

"Si, sergeanto."

"The señora wants to take many photos of Panama hats, how they are made and sold. Comprende?"

"Yes, I know most of the ladies here who make those things."

"Okay, then, let's get going."

The three got up and walked to the edge of the plaza, which was lined with small shops, almost identical in layout: a sales counter in front, the main shop full of hats, and in the back, two or three women making the hats.

For the next four hours, Maxine alternately photographed and talked to these women about the hats. How were they made and of what material? How many did they sell and who bought them? Were the hats exported? In each case, Tito would walk in first, say a few words, and then beckon Maxine and Grogan forward so she could begin her work.

It was magical for Maxine: the white hats set against the brown faces, together with the old buildings around the plaza. Two of the businesses were supported by her client, the International Business Consortium. She spent more time with those proprietors, taking a lot of notes and photos for the report she would be writing to complete her assignment.

As she did her work, Grogan and Tito followed but stayed outside the various shops. She could see them talking and laughing and thoroughly enjoying each other's company.

When the bells on the nearby church tolled at noon, Maxine walked over and sat down next to them. "Wow! What a great place for a photographer. I got incredible images. Do you like my hat? I bought it at the last store I visited." She posed like a model, taking her new Panama hat with a purple band on and off and bowing to them. They laughed and Tito clapped. "But I'm tired. I need some food and something to drink."

"I can take care of that," said Grogan. "Tito, let's go get some food for the *señora*."

As the two of them walked away, Maxine saw four men enter the plaza on the opposite side. Even from a distance, there was no mistaking the man in the lead: Seth Barlow. The other three were the same Chinese thugs who were at the plane and had killed Inez. How had he found her?

She put on her dark glasses, pulled her hat down over her face, and got up. Then she took her camera straps from around her neck and shoved the cameras into her backpack. She edged her way around the plaza toward Grogan and the boy, pretending to look at the various wares spread out on tables. Because the stalls were surrounded by gauzy curtains, it was easy to hide. The last stall was near to where Grogan and Tito were paying for the food. The sergeant looked up and saw Maxine. He smiled but then frowned when he saw her face. She pointed to where Barlow and the others were still standing, and he glanced in that direction. He edged toward her slowly, pulling his gun.

"Tito, I want you to put down the food and take the *señora* by the hand and lead her away from here. *Comprende?*"

The boy looked confused at first, then seemed to sense the danger. "Is this a mission, *sergeanto?* Like you told me about?"

"Yes, that is what it is, Tito. Our mission. And you cannot fail me, right partner?"

"I will never fail you, *sergeanto,*" said Tito, looking up at the big man gravely.

"Okay, let's move."

"Where will you be?" asked Maxine.

"Right behind you," said Grogan. "Now go!"

Tito and Maxine moved along the various stalls until they reached the other side of the plaza.

Just then, Maxine heard Seth Barlow's voice. "THERE SHE IS! GO GET HER!"

She grabbed Tito and crouched down behind a wall.

"I DON'T THINK SO, BARLOW!" Grogan shouted. "You are a disgrace to your country. You are a traitor. Drop your gun and get your Chinese goons to do the same."

Barlow laughed and nodded to the other men. One pulled out a gun and shot the sergeant in the chest. People in the plaza screamed and dove for cover, sending Panama hats flying.

"*Sergeanto, sergeanto.* No, no, no!" Tito broke free of Maxine's grip and raced to the dying man. The other men stepped aside and let the boy get close to Grogan.

The boy cradled the sergeant's head in his arms and rocked back and forth. "No, no, no," he sobbed, tears streaming down his cheeks. "*Mi amigo, mi amigo!*"

"And who is this little mongrel?" hissed Barlow. "Looks like the good sergeant's been getting a little on the side. Ha, ha, ha, ha."

At that point, Maxine was ready to stand up and run to them, Seth Barlow be damned, but strong brown arms restrained her. Two of the hat makers she had interviewed earlier, Rosa and Maria, led her away to the next street and into a building filled with Panama hats. They led Maxine up a ladder to a loft.

"Rest now, *señora*," said one of the women, who looked to be in her fifties. "I will bring the boy to you after the men have gone."

"But is he safe, that dear little Tito?"

"That boy has nine lives like a cat," she said, smiling. "I think he will be okay."

Maxine cried herself to sleep, thinking about the friends she'd lost and wondering how she would ever get out of this tiny town in this remote country.

Maxine woke up in the middle of the night when she heard someone climbing the stairs. Rosa and Tito climbed the ladder and stepped into the loft. Tito ran to her.

"*Señora, señora,* I have lost my only friend," the boy sobbed. "What will I do?"

Maxine pulled him toward her and hugged him tightly, but that made him cry even harder.

"I know, I know. I am so sorry. He was my friend too. He was very brave. He tried to stop those men from getting to me." She brushed away his tears with her hand. "How did you get away? Did the men hurt you?"

"Naw," he said, "I was brave too. I told them to leave me alone and they did. I guess they thought I know nothing."

"Did they just leave?"

"I think so. I sat with the *sergeanto* for a long time, and then some of the men in the town carried him into the church. The doctor came and the priest and they are standing guard."

"I need to do something to get him out of here," said Maxine. "I need to be brave too."

"He had this in his backpack." Tito handed Maxine something she remembered seeing Grogan use earlier. It was his satellite phone. But how to use it?

She stood up and fooled around with the dials, and it soon came to life. Grogan had it set on one frequency. "Hello. Can anyone hear me? I am an American citizen, and I need help."

"Who is speaking, please?" said a male voice.

"My name is Maxine March, and I am in Montecristi, Ecuador. I was with Sergeant Grogan, but I am afraid he has been killed."

"Say no more, Ms. March," said the voice. "We will be there as soon as we can. We have you on our coordinates."

Tito stayed with Maxine while they waited. They talked about their lives, and the hard time he and his family had always had. She talked about her adventures all over the world taking photos.

"Really, you saw polar bears?" His eyes were bright at the thought. "And icebergs? ¡Que bueno!"

Then he fell asleep, his head in her lap. She dozed on and off, and then awakened with a start at the sound of a helicopter. Tito jumped to his feet. "The good guys are here to save us!" he shouted.He grabbed her hand, and they climbed down the ladder. He seemed to know where the helicopter had landed and ran up the hill to an empty field, pulling her along behind him.

The small chopper landed softly, stirring up the dust of the field and shaking the ground all around it. Maxine and Tito crouched behind some large boulders until the rotors had stopped turning, then they stood up as the side door opened and a familiar figure jumped onto the ground.

"I knew you were crazy about me," Paul Bickford said to Maxine, "but this is a pretty extreme way to get my attention."

"You bastard, Paul. I'm sure you say that to all the girls," she replied. Then she put her arm around Tito. "Colonel Paul Bickford, this is a very brave young man, Tito Morales. He has been a great assistant to Sergeant Grogan for many years."

Tito saluted the tall officer and bowed.

"My distinct honor, sir," Bickford shook his hand. "You are very brave indeed. Sergeant Grogan told me about you."

"He did?" said Tito proudly. Then he grabbed Bickford around legs and hugged him as he had Grogan. Maxine burst into tears at the memory.

"Okay, my little man, can you take me to where the sergeant is? It will be your last mission for him."

"Yes, sir. Please follow me."

"Maxie, get into the chopper. I'll get your stuff for you, and we'll be back in a few minutes. Lead the way, Tito."

The boy took Bickford by the hand, and they started walking back to the plaza. Before long, Bickford picked the boy up and carried him.

Maxine was helped into the aircraft by two men who were dressed in desert camouflage, as was Bickford. In a few minutes Bickford returned, carrying the body of Grogan in his arms, Tito walking close behind. The others loaded the body and all of their packs into the chopper.

Bickford held back his emotions as he had trained himself to do for years—Maxine was not so constrained. She jumped down and stood next to Bickford, then knelt down at Tito's side.

"I hate to leave you, Tito," she sobbed. "I love you, and I wish you were my little boy. You are so strong and brave. I know the *sergeanto* would be very proud of you." She handed him some cash, all she had left of her expense money.

Bickford reached into his wallet and did the same. "For services rendered to the United States of America," he said. He saluted and so did Tito as he accepted it.

"Goodbye my little pal," cried Maxine.

She turned and followed Bickford into the helicopter. As it took off, she had a last look at Tito as he maintained his salute for a long time, but then collapsed onto the ground, his body shaking with sobs.

86

TOM

MAXINE'S MESSAGE HAD BEEN TERSE: "Meet me at Portland air base, July 1, about 10 a.m. Give name at gate." All the way to Portland I had wondered why she was coming back from Ecuador in a military plane. Leave it to Maxine to finagle a free ride.

I made good time and arrived at the base in two and a half hours. I drove up and an airman walked up to the car. "Yes, sir. How can I help?"

"I'm meeting a military plane that is supposed to be coming in from South America. A friend is on board. She or someone was supposed to make arrangements to get me in."

"May I see some identification?"

I pulled out my wallet, removed my driver's license, and handed it to him.

"Give me a moment, sir." The young airman walked to the small building next to the gate and picked up a phone. When he returned to the car, he said, "You are cleared to enter. Please drive over to that parking lot and someone will meet you."

"Thank you."

The gate opened, and I drove through to the parking lot. Another airman waited there and pointed to an empty space at the end of a row of government vehicles. He approached the car as I opened the door and got out.

"Mr. Martin . . ."

"Martindale."

"Sorry I didn't get your name right."

"No problem, sergeant."

"Please follow me to the waiting area. The plane should be here within a half-hour."

The sergeant had long legs so I had to pick up the pace to keep up with him. We walked around the building to an area next to the runway.

"Sergeant, I have a question."

"Yes, sir. I will answer it if I can."

"Where is this plane coming from? What kind of a plane is it—I mean, is it from the military or some other government agency?"

"I'm afraid I am not at liberty to divulge that information, sir."

"What can you tell me, then?"

He looked at his clipboard. "Among the passengers is a civilian, Ms. Maxine March. That's about it, sir."

"That's a relief. She's the friend I'm meeting. Is anyone else listed on your manifest?"

"I am not at liberty to say, sir."

"Or where it's coming from?"

He shook his head.

"I know the drill. Loose lips sink ships." I smiled, but the young sergeant did not.

"I beg your pardon, sir?"

"Oh, it's an old expression," I said, laughing. "You're too young to have heard it. It means you shouldn't say anything when you're in a crowd because the wrong people might hear it."

He looked perplexed. "If you say so, sir."

Just then, I heard the high-pitched whine of a small jet, and we both turned to watch it touch down softly, its tires squealing as the reverse thrust of the engines slowed it down. It taxied toward us and turned. In a couple minutes, the door opened and a stairway unfolded. Two female air force stewards got off and turned to help the passengers disembark.

First to come off was an older officer with the chest full of medals to go with the two stars on his shoulder boards. The airmen—air ladies?—saluted. He got into a waiting car, and it quickly drove off.

Maxine was next, and she looked terrible. Her clothes were dirty and her hair looked as if it had not been washed in weeks. I started to wave to her and then saw the next person to get off. I had hoped never to see Paul Bickford again, but there he was in all his starched army glory. Even though he was in full camouflage, I could see the sharp creases on both his shirt and his pants. He also saluted the ladies at the stairway, then he whispered something to Maxine, and she looked at me.

"Hello, Maxine. Hello, Paul. I didn't think we'd ever meet again," I shouted over the noise of the engines. Kind of a bland line for such a momentous and, for me anyway, hurtful reunion. I just stood there, trying to figure out what this meant.

"Hello, Tom," Maxine said, after a few more awkward moments. She walked over to me and gave me a very glancing peck on the cheek.

I shook her hand and turned to Paul. "You do manage to turn up in odd places."

"It's part of my game—to keep everyone off balance," he said. He put out his hand and I shook it without hesitation, then he turned to the sergeant. "Is there any place we can talk privately, sergeant?"

"Yes, Colonel. Please follow me." He led the way to another building and opened the door by punching in a combination. "This is a secure room, sir. I have taken the liberty of having coffee brought in." He stepped aside and we entered.

"Thank you, sergeant." Bickford said. "I very much appreciate your work here, and I will be letting Colonel Masters know how much."

"Yes, sir. Thank you, sir." The young sergeant saluted and closed the door.

"God, I feel like I'm a hundred years old," Maxine announced. "I'm sure I look it too. I haven't had a bath in days or even put on makeup. I'm going to see what I can resurrect of my face." She got up and walked to the nearby bathroom.

Bickford and I sat down at opposite sides of the table after he had poured two cups of coffee.

I cleared my throat. "I'm kind of in shock here. I mean, seeing you and the two of you together," I said. "Don't get me wrong. Anything she and I had together was finished out there at the lighthouse those many years ago. What is it? Four or five?"

"God, I don't know, Tom," he said, wearily. "I lose track of days and weeks, so you can't expect me to remember years." He rubbed his face with his hands.

"So, behind the spit and polish, there is a human being in there who gets tired and thirsty and hungry," I said.

"You bet. The spit and polish is what's holding me together."

This was a more casual Bickford than I had ever seen before. I decided this might be a good time to get more information from him. At this point, I didn't know anything. "So, can you tell me what this is all about? Or is it classified like everything you do always is—including your promotion to Colonel, which you've failed to tell me about?!"

"Promotions go with the territory, you know that. As far as this situation with Maxine, I have been cleared to tell you some of it," he said. "But let's wait until she gets back out here." He put his coffee cup on the table. "What happened, happened to her. I just came in at the end to try to pick up the pieces."

At that moment, Maxine walked out of the bathroom. "Whew! I feel just a little bit better. But I still look like hell. I've got to have a shower and buy some clothes."

Bickford poured her some coffee as she sat down at the table.

"You look good, Tom," said Maxine.

"Yeah, I feel pretty good for an old guy."

"I guess you want to know what this is all about," she said, smiling. "I owe it to you since you might become involved."

"I'm all ears."

For the next hour or so, Maxine told me the story of her trip to Ecuador. Meeting Seth Barlow on the plane, what he did to her, about her friend Inez Santiago-Verde, and the trip into the jungle. And then seeing Barlow with the Chinese men, Barlow's pursuit of them, and Inez's death.

At that point in her story, she started to cry. "She was a good friend and a great journalist. She didn't deserve to die at the hands of a scumbag like Barlow."

Bickford reached across the table and patted her hand. I looked away.

Maxine resumed her story and told how she contacted Bickford using an old number that was still working. "It was his old number, Tom. We haven't talked in several years."

I waved away the comment. "Go on with your story."

She told me about Sergeant Grogan and her determination to finish her assignment by talking him into taking her to Montecristi. "If I hadn't insisted, he'd be alive now," she sobbed again. "He was such a good man." Then she talked about a little Ecuadorian boy named Tito and cried harder. "What a wonderful little fellow. I would love to adopt him."

Bickford then told his part of the story, about how he had been nearby and was able to get a helicopter to come to her rescue.

I thought to myself, how could anyone like me ever hope to compete with that kind of resourcefulness and bravery?

"God, Paul, you get helicopters like the rest of us rent cars."

He shrugged. "What can I say? It's what I do." Bickford looked at the two of us, with a serious look on his face. "Bottom line for the two of you: Seth Barlow may be able to track you here, Maxie. Apparently he's gone rogue, and a rogue agent can be like a wounded animal. Very dangerous. You saw what caused him to compromise his career and betray his country—he's working with the Chinese on their oil deal with the Ecuadorians. You saw him meeting with them, and Inez took photos of it. He thinks you have her camera and the photos."

"I haven't even looked at what is in the camera," she said. "There are thousands of photos."

"You need to give me the camera, so I can get those images analyzed," said Bickford.

"But they're Inez's work. I owe it to her to get them published. I thought I'd send them to her editors in Madrid or London or wherever they are."

"Whoa, now," said Bickford, holding up both hands. "You need to step back from this and think of it not like a journalist but like a citizen. Your government saved you. I saved you. And the payment is whatever photos you have of Barlow."

"I hate it when you pull out your patriot card," she said. "You sounded like Dick Cheney just then." She fumbled with the three cameras in her bag and pulled out one of them. "Okay, okay. I surrender. I know you saved my life."

"You bet your sweet ass I did," he said, laughing while putting the camera she gave him into his briefcase. "I've got to go. All I can say to the two of you is to be careful. I don't really think Barlow can track you here, but you never know. Finish your assignment and get back to New York; I'll keep in touch. In the meantime, I'll try to figure out where Barlow is. If he is CIA, which I am sure he is, I'll let his bosses find him and arrest him. Those photos will be the proof they need." Bickford stood up and shook my hand, then he hugged Maxine.

"Thank you, Paul," she said. "As always, you were my rescuer."

Bickford walked out the door and toward the jet, which was revving up its engines. The two of us sat and drank coffee and listened as the small craft taxied to the end of the runway and took off.

"Can we get out of here and go buy me some clothes?" Maxine asked.

As we walked to the door, Maxine paused and pulled out one of the cameras. She checked it quickly and put it away.

"You didn't give him the right camera, did you?" I asked her.

"Inez deserves to have her work in print. And it's up to me to see that the world knows what is happening in Ecuador. I don't want to have her photos buried in some secret government archive, with so many levels of classification that they never see the light of day."

TOM AND MAXINE

WE DIDN'T REACH THE OREGON COAST until after dark. I stopped at the Woodburn Mall so Maxine could buy clothes in its many shops. Like a bored husband or boyfriend, I waited outside at each establishment. Each time she emerged, she handed me another bag to carry.

"I love doing this, Tom. I haven't done such a girlie thing in years. I rarely have to dress up any more. If I go on the job dressed like a fashion model, people tend to look at me when I'm trying to blend into the woodwork. No one pays any attention to a dumpy photographer who looks like one of the guys."

We stopped for dinner in Salem and didn't reach her hotel until eight that night.

"It's a really nice place," I said, as we drove down the steeply inclined driveway of the Inn at Spanish Head. "The hotel is built into the side of a cliff. You enter on the top floor and then take an elevator down to your room. And each one has a view of the ocean."

"Wonderful, Tom, but I don't have much of an expense account. *Smithsonian* is not *Vanity Fair* or *Vogue*."

"Don't worry about it," I said. "One of my friends has a unit here, so you will be his guest and only have to pay the few incidental charges. It's an owner-occupied place."

As we pulled up, one of the valets ran over to my car. "Checking in, sir and madam?"

"My friend has a reservation. Can I leave my car here for a few minutes while I get her settled in?"

"Of course, sir. Pop the trunk, and I'll get the bags."

I did, and he walked around to the rear of the car. Maxine got out of the car, clutching her large handbag.

"I remember how you always protected your Leica camera when we first met," I said.

"It was the only thing of value I had," she said, shaking her head. "That's still my best camera, and I still use it, like in Ecuador; however, digital saves time because you don't need to develop film. It's very sad when the old is replaced by the new—in this case, a flashier and quicker new."

We walked into the pleasant lobby, and I told the clerk about the room arrangement. Maxine signed in and got the key card for her room as the valet carried in her bag.

"I can manage from here, Tom," Maxine said. "Can I rent a car anywhere?"

"The carnival is within walking distance, so maybe you won't need a car. Why don't I pick you up for breakfast and then take you to the carnival to introduce you?"

"Okay, Tom. You're the boss," she said, smiling. "See you in the morning."

As I walked back outside and got in my car, I felt relieved that my first meeting with Maxine after so long had gone so well. It would be nice to be friends again and forget all the bad stuff that had happened between us. When I think I've been betrayed by someone, that person normally vanishes from my memory, but given the circumstances, I might have to make an exception in Maxine's case. And it would be nice to have her nearby, even if only for a few days.

★ ★ ★ ★ ★

We dropped by Captain Dan's Pirate Pastry the next morning, shortly after nine.

"How arrrrrrrr ya?" shouted Dan from the back.

"You can cut the pirate talk, Dan, it's only me."

"Oh, too bad my accent was wasted on the old," he said. "But who is this pretty lass you have brought into my clutches? Are you ready to walk the plank with me?"

Maxine smiled but looked a bit startled.

"Don't worry," said Dan's wife from behind the table where she was preparing the pastry. "He's harmless." She walked over and hugged me.

"Dan and Kathy, this is my friend Maxine March, the photographer I told you about. She's the one who's going to be taking photos around the carnival."

"Good to meet you," said Dan. "Welcome to our humble abode." Then he bowed.

"Cut the slapstick, Dan, and get us some food!" I said.

"Right you are, my hearty bucko."

Maxine and I walked over to the pastry case. "Wow, it all looks good," said Maxine. "I'll have one of each. Not really. How about an apple turnover and one of those scones."

"The same for me," I said. "And coffees."

"Do you have chai tea?" asked Maxine.

"We do," answered Kathy. "I'll get your drinks."

97

Dan led us to a table near the front window, where the traffic on Highway 101 rushed by. "I can sit with you for a minute since we aren't very busy this morning. So, Tom tells me you're a really good photographer, Maxine. It must be hard to make a living at doing only that, even if you are good."

"Yes, you are right about that," she said, between bites of her turnover. "It's very hard now and getting worse all the time. With so much online now, print publications like I used to work for are cutting back or going out of business altogether. I can't afford to turn down any assignment."

"Maxine just got back from Ecuador on assignment for a non-profit organization," I said. "The photos are for their use, like in PR and marketing stuff, not for the media at all."

Just then the door opened and a young couple with three small children came into the shop. Dan got up and walked behind the counter. "How arrrrrrr ya?" he shouted.

One of the kids, a little girl, started to cry.

"The captain didn't mean to scare you," Dan said with a guilty look on his face.

"Do it again!" shouted the girl's brother, as he ran over to a bin of stuffed animals wearing pirate outfits and dumped them all on the floor.

TOM AND MAXINE

AFTER EATING, WE SAID GOODBYE to Kathy and Dan and drove down to the end of 53rd Street where the carnival was already set up. Maxine got out of the car and started snapping photos as we walked onto the grounds. When she ducked under a rope, a tough-looking guy with a shaved head and tattoos on his muscular arms came running over to us.

"We're not open yet," he said. "You'll have to wait until noon."

Maxine aimed her camera at him and took several shots.

"Wait. What the fuck are you doin'?" He tried to knock her camera to the ground, but I stepped between them.

"You wait," I said. "We've got permission from Hank Carson to be here. Is he here?"

The man stepped back and stopped trying to grab Maxine's camera.

"It's okay, Vinny, I know all about this."

We turned to see a man dressed in a clown suit walking toward us. With his painted-on sad face, it was hard to tell who he was. I have always been afraid of clowns. As a kid going to the circus, I avoided them and didn't join in the laughter of the other kids at the clowns' often outrageous antics. But I loved the trapeze artists and the lion tamer.

The clown walked briskly to us and stuck out his hand. "Father Eddie, at your service. Mr. Martin, was it?"

"Close enough. Nice to see you again, even in your clown suit. I thought you were a man of the cloth. You obviously have other talents."

Of course, Maxine had started taking photos of the clown immediately. He did not seem to care.

"I have always loved clowns, so Hank lets me dress up once in a while, especially if we are short-handed. So I'm a substitute clown when needed. A few of them have not arrived yet, so here I am."

"Father Eddie, this is the photographer friend I told you and Mr. Carson about, Maxine March."

"My honor, Miss March. I have looked you up online," he said. "You are a great photographer."

"Thank you. I appreciate the compliment. I try my best, but the cameras do all the real work. I just point and shoot."

"Hardly that, Maxie," I added. "You need the right 'eye' to pick your shots."

"I like that term, the photographer's 'eye'," said the priest. "Very descriptive of what you do and your skill at doing it."

"So, Father Eddie, I brought Maxine here to look things over and to meet you and Mr. Carson. Is he here?"

"I think so. Let me check his office and tell him you're here."

"Nice man," said Maxine, as he walked away from us.

"Not so great, according to some background stuff I got from a reporter friend of mine in Cleveland. He was thrown out of the church for molesting a couple of choir boys, which he denied, of course. He met Hank at church and they teamed up together. I guess he's Hank's right-hand man around the carnival. Not sure how the church would feel about him still wearing his priest collar, but I would imagine it gives a certain cachet to both of them."

"What about Hank Carson?" asked Maxine. "What unsavory stuff did you find out about him?"

"Hard to know where to be . . ."

"Mr. Martin and Miss March," yelled Father Eddie from down the Midway. "Mr. Carson will see you now. Step right this way, as we say in the carnival business."

TOM AND MAXINE

The motor home/office was luxurious inside, like I imagined one of those movie star's dressing rooms might be. The paneled walls were covered with framed photos of carnival scenes and, I presume, carnival performers Carson had known and worked with. The carpet looked expensive, as did the leather and chrome furniture.

As I had seen from outside a few weeks before, his desk was on a raised platform so Carson would be looking down upon—and thus dominating—anyone standing in front of him. Mr. Rambo, the parrot, was sitting on its perch to the left of the desk, seemingly with its eyes closed. Bird seed, feathers, and no small amount of bird droppings littered the carpet in an arc out from the parrot's perch.

"Welcome to my humble abode," said Carson in a raspy voice. "Excuse my voice. I sometimes get colds when we're on the road."

As Maxine and I reached up to shake Carson's hand, the parrot began to screech, "PRETTY GIRL, PRETTY GIRL."

"How nice," said Maxine. "I've never been complimented by a parrot before."

"He likes pretty women," said Carson, who kept Maxine's hand in his a bit longer than necessary.

"We don't want to take too much of your time," I said. "I just wanted to introduce you to Maxine. As you recall, you gave her permission to take photos around the carnival. I assume she has the freedom to do that without anyone hassling her."

Carson's eyes flashed. "My people do not *hassle*, as you so indelicately put it, Mr. Martin."

"Poor choice of words," I said. "Sorry. I just meant that when you're on assignment, people who do not know why you're where you are sometimes try to stop you from doing your job. I was a journalist, and I've been in that position more than once."

Carson reached into a drawer and pulled out something encased in plastic. He handed it to Eddie, who was standing next to him. Eddie handed it to Maxine.

"Great. A press pass. That will work well. Thank you." She slipped the lanyard that the pass was attached to over her head.

"As I understand from Mr. Martin here, you are taking photos of our workers. And it is for *National Geographic*. I have been reading that fine magazine all my life. I remember that my grandmother used to keep stacks . . ."

"*Smithsonian*, not *National Geographic*," corrected Maxine.

"What?"

"I said, I'm working for a different magazine. It is published by the Smithsonian Institution in Washington, D.C."

"Never heard of it," said Carson with a shrug.

"I assure you, it is a fine magazine," Maxine said. "It does publish articles that are similar to those in *National Geographic*."

"What do you think we should do, Mr. Rambo?" said Carson, turning to the parrot. "Should we let this nice lady in on all of our secrets?"

"PRETTY GIRL, PRETTY GIRL," shrieked the parrot.

"I'll take that as a 'yes'," Maxine said, smiling. "I'd love to start right here and shoot some photos of you, Mr. Carson," she said, eager to get on with her work.

Carson turned to me. "Did you tell her that I want approval over every photo she takes?"

I looked at Maxine, who shook her head. No journalist would consent to that.

"Let's work that out later, "I said to Carson, who smiled and stood up, all five feet of him. He reached for a mirror and looked at his gnarled face, then ran a comb through his hair and put on a cowboy hat with a silver band. Finally, he stepped down from the platform with Eddie's help.

Maxine stepped closer and started snapping away, the whir of the shutter the only sound in the room. Carson kept turning his head as if he thought he had a good side.

"Just keep walking," Maxine said. "Maybe go on outside so I can see you in action."

Carson smiled, probably liking the use of that word to indicate how much in charge of things he was. He and Eddie started walking up the Midway toward the entrance. The various workers they passed stopped what they were doing and turned to nod at him or, in the case of an older man, take off his hat.

Maxine ran ahead of them and kept shooting while trying different angles. At one point, Carson stopped to talk to five burly men who were setting up the infamous Zipper.

"A moment, please," he said, turning to us. Following that cue, we walked away from him and Eddie as they talked in hushed tones to the workers. Carson did most of the talking, gesturing and pointing at the large superstructure of the ride.

"I'll bet they make most of their money on that thing," I said to Maxine. "I've always hated heights. I went on a roller coaster once and that was enough." I looked at the cages that would rattle around the structure—the bars reminded me of the parrot's cage. "The merry-go-round is more my style."

"I guess I was a bit more adventuresome than you," she said. "I went on roller coasters a lot as a kid, usually on a dare from boyfriends." She winked and went on with her work, taking photos of the overall scene. The Midway was taking shape quickly with brightly colored tents and stalls going up along each side.

"Do you feel comfortable enough for me to leave now?" I asked her. "I've got some errands to run and need to get home to call my agent."

"Sure, Tom," she said. "What can happen to me here with all these people around? I'll stay for a couple of hours, trying to see who I want to feature and talking to them."

"Just promise me you'll watch out for Mr. Rambo," I said, laughing. "He's got the hots for you big time."

MAXINE

MAXINE SPENT THE REST OF THE DAY walking around the carnival grounds, constantly taking photos and talking to various workers. After a while, she began to feel good about her assignment and that she would probably be able to finish it easily. She had been away from New York for almost a month and was eager to get back into her old life as a big city professional.

The people she stopped to photograph and talk to were, for the most part, very nice. She got out her small tape recorder and placed it on any nearby surface. No one objected when she turned it on. The stories they told were as interesting as the way they looked.

Marge Daniels — "I've been fat all my life. Honey, I can't tell you how many diets I've been on over the years. A couple of years ago, I decided to try to make my weight pay off for me. No more diets. As if on cue, my body seemed to think that was great, so here I am, all three hundred pounds of me. I try to stay healthy and dress well. You know, most fat women just give up on trying to look good, but you can still retain some elegance with the right clothes and the right makeup. I just let it all hang out, so to speak, and the customers seem to like it. I know my boyfriend does. That's him over there, the skinny guy. He says there is more of me to love. And, honey, let me tell you, my weight doesn't stand in the way of having good sex with him."

Leroy Anders—"I'm in charge of the animals we have around here. Since this isn't a circus, we don't have big animals, just some ponies for the kids to ride and animals for the petting zoo—mice, a llama, some rabbits, a hamster, snakes, a couple of goats, two pigs, and a sheep—that sort of thing. Oh yeah, we've also got a few spiders under glass over there in that case. Not too poisonous!" He smiled at Maxine, and she took a number of images of his face. She was especially fascinated by a whole row of gold teeth. "I love life on the road. I've been in my share of trouble in the past so sometimes it's nice to be able to get out of town, if you get my drift."

Elmer "Ace" St. Romaine—"I've always hated the name Elmer so I've called myself Ace most of my life. I think it fits me better, don't you? I mean, I don't look like an Elmer. Don't you agree? I'm not bad looking but the gals turn and walk the other way if I tell them my name is Elmer. Jesus H. Christ. That's a sissy name. I learned to swallow swords from my uncle who was a carnie for years and years. It's a secret, how I do it, but I could show you how if you care to come to my trailer when I get off work."

Monte Gable—"Marge and me's been friends and lovers for a long time. I love that big gal more than I can say. There is so much of her to love. I'm the thin man who *stands next to her as the fat lady. Neat contrast, don't you think? I wear a tuxedo to match her evening gown. We talk to the people as they walk by, mostly to get them to go into the tent to see the man wrestling the alligator and the octopus. We charge extra for that. I guess we're kind of like shills, getting folks to part with extra money beyond what they've already paid to get onto the Midway. Marge and me, we share a trailer, and I love being able to spend so much time in her company. You know, she's real smart. Got her AA degree in cosmetology a while back. Her dream is to open her own beauty shop or a spa maybe. Not sure what I'd do, but she'll figure something out. She's real smart."*

Gordy Hargraves—*"I come from a long line of clowns. I mean, they've been in my family for years. My uncle appeared with Emmett Kelly in the Ringling Brothers shows for many years. That's the best you can do in this business. He died a few years back. I wanted to get a job with Ringling, but they said I wasn't funny enough or sad enough. That's all done with how we make up our faces. I prefer to be sad because that's the way I usually feel. But if Mr. Carson told me tomorrow to become a happy clown, I'd be able to do it. I am* versa-tile, *no doubt about it."*

Madame Wellington—*"There have been a lot of gypsy fortune-tellers in the news lately. We are from the Romany people. Do you know what that means? It means we are like a tribe that began centuries ago. Because of our dark looks and bad reputations—not deserved at all—we have been cast aside by many countries in Europe. So* *that has made us nomads. We travel from country to country, searching for ways to make a living. We do help each other and stick together. Safety in numbers, I believe you call it. We are not hounded so much in the United States. Some of us steal and rob people and maybe get into gangs like the mafia. Our men like to buy and sell cars. Lots of money in that, believe me. Others of us, like yours truly, trade on our exotic beauty. Do you like my nice skin? I use a lot of creams and spend a lot of money on makeup. Nice, don't you think? I tell fortunes by reading a person's palms. No crystal balls for me. That is ridiculous. I don't do séances either. That's impossible. But looking at someone's palms is a sure way to look into their souls. Stick out your hands, and I'll tell you what's next for you. Don't be afraid."*

TOM

MAXINE CALLED ME THAT NIGHT just as I finished unpacking the last box of my books. I love the feel of real books and will probably never replace them with e-books, but they are a pain when it comes to moving. I moved fifty boxes into my new loft study and was just barely able to fit them all into the shelves.

"Hi, Tom. Just wanted to report about my day," she said. "I got off to a good start, I think. No one hassled me and I was able to get some good stuff, both in brief interviews and in the images I took."

"Great. I'm glad. There did seem to be a lot of people around with interesting faces."

"Let's see, I talked to the fat lady, her thin boyfriend, a sword-swallower, another clown, an animal guy, and a gypsy fortune-teller, Madame Wellington. Isn't that fun? I'm enjoying the contrast to what I usually do. These people lead interesting lives."

"Sounds like it," I said. "So what's next?"

"I think I can wind it up with one more day of shooting and get on my way."

"Okay, that's great. I'm sure you'll be happy to get home. How long have you been on the road?"

"Counting my time in Ecuador, almost three weeks. I need to get on with my life."

The thought crossed my mind that I should ask Maxine to stay around a little longer, maybe try to repair our friendship a bit more. But I dismissed it. What happened between us was a long time ago, and it was more than enough that we were back on speaking terms.

"I'll let you go, Tom. I need to take a shower and get some rest. I still feel like I've got Ecuadorian jungle smells in my clothes."

"Thanks for calling, Maxie. Get some sleep." I paused, wondering if I should at least be more hospitable without her thinking I was aiming for something more. "Maxine, want to have lunch tomorrow?"

"No, I don't think so. I need to go over my shots and delete the bad images. Also, a new clown is supposed to be arriving, and I want to spend some time with him. I think the three clowns will be the anchors for my piece—'the sadness behind the happy face.' That sort of thing. A cliché but an effective one, I think."

I was deflated but didn't let it show in my voice. "Okay. Great. Keep in touch. Good night."

And that, as they say, was that.

MAXINE

MAXINE SPENT THE MORNING IN HER HOTEL ROOM, organizing her images and notes and listening to the tapes of her interviews. She was pleased with the results: strong photos of people with very interesting faces and all of them with good stories to tell. She suspected that her final story would lean heavily on the photos, with the words used only to explain the photos—a photo essay as it used to be called in the quickly vanishing old days of journalism.

At noon, she left the room and walked to the carnival grounds, which were gradually coming to life. This was opening day so there was more bustle than there had been the day before. Carnies were raking the sawdust on the paths and proprietors were arranging their games and tightening the poles of their open-front tents. Maxine photographed them all as she walked down the Midway.

At the far end, ten workers were maneuvering the Zipper into its final position. Eddie was standing next to a man dressed in a suit and holding a clipboard. When Maxine aimed her camera in their direction, Eddie put up his hand to stop her and quickly walked over to her.

"This guy's the state inspector," he whispered. "Better not distract him, if you don't mind. The Zipper is the big one for us, but it's also the one that has lots of safety issues. We spend more time worrying about it than anything else in the show." Eddie turned his attention back to the maniacal machine. "But it brings in a lot of money. Beats me how people want to be scared and are willing to pay for it."

"Eddie, is there any time today that I could talk to Mr. Carson?"

"What about? He's kind of reluctant to be quoted. He likes me to handle that kind of thing for him. Can I help?"

"Well, sure. I guess. I only wanted to ask him why he thinks people get into this business. I'd call it kind of a summing-up quote. I've talked to some of your people and I'll put their quotes with their photos, but I want something else to go with it."

"I see what you're aiming at. Better to come from him. Let me ask him. I need to follow this inspector around and then I'll go see Hank. He'll be up by then—he's a night owl." As Eddie started to walk away, he stopped and looked behind Maxine. "Oh, here's Gordy with our newest clown. He got in last night. Gordy, come on over and introduce our new guy to Miss March."

"Miss March, this is our newest clown, Andy Dumas," said Gordy. "He hails from California."

The new man had a red clown mask on and it was, to her, somewhat scary: a snarly mouth with jagged teeth, a pointed nose, extra-large and pointed ears, horns, and eyes shrouded by low brows. Dumas extended his hand and Maxine shook it. His shake was limp and tentative and his palms sweaty.

"Hello. Good to meet you," said Maxine.

Dumas bowed but didn't say anything. He pointed to his throat and shook his head.

"Andy's picked up laryngitis, but since clowns don't have to say anything, he'll be able to help us out," said Gordy.

"What happened to your regular guy?" asked Maxine.

"Not really sure," said Eddie. "Burt, that's his name, was supposed to arrive yesterday and when he didn't, I called the company where we get our clowns. They didn't know where he was either. Fortunately, they sent us Andy."

Eddie walked over and patted Andy on the back. Andy pulled away a bit and did not seem to like the familiarity.

"I have to say that Burt had a bit of a drinking problem so I'm not all that surprised," Eddie continued.

"But he always called me," said Gordy, shaking his head. "Not like him to disrespect us like that. Oh well, I guess there's a first time for everything."

"So, he wasn't in your usual troop? I mean, he didn't travel all over the country with you?" asked Maxine.

"No. Except for Gordy here, we find it better to hire clowns in each state we're in," said Eddie. "That way we get a variety of looks and don't have to provide accommodations for travel."

"Speaking of looks," said Maxine, "I don't think I've ever seen a clown with a devil face. Doesn't it scare the kiddies?"

At that point, Andy Dumas raised both hands and made his fingers into claws and pretended to lunge at Maxine.

"God, you scared me!" She stepped back in surprise. "Please don't do that again."

"And don't do it with any kids," said Eddie, a look of alarm on his face. "Okay?"

Dumas bowed, shook his head, and shrugged his shoulders.

"We'd better start rehearsing," said Gordy, taking Dumas by the arm and guiding him away from Maxine and Eddie.

When they were out of earshot, Maxine turned to Eddie. "That guy's kind of scary."

"I think so too," he replied. "I'll keep my eye on him and get one of my guys to watch him too. I just can't figure out what happened to Burt."

Maxine did not see either clown for the next few hours, as she wandered around the Midway talking to people and taking photo after photo. At one o'clock, people started walking into the Midway to see the show. At first they came in a trickle and then, after about a half-hour, there were so many people, Maxine nearly got lost in the crowd.

At three, Eddie joined her and whispered, "Hank's got a few minutes to see you now. I'll take you to his office."

Because of the press of people around them, it took a long time to reach the motor home. Eddie stepped up to the door and knocked.

"It's open," shouted Carson.

Eddie stood aside and helped Maxine up the wooden steps. "I'll leave the two of you to talk," he said. "I'll be back in a half-hour. Will that be enough time?"

"More than enough. Thanks."

The lights in the room were turned so low that Maxine could barely see once she was inside.

"Come on in, sweetie," said Carson. "I'm over here, next to my desk."

No one had called her that in years, and she didn't much like it, but sources are sources and she needed to finish her assignment.

"Mr. Carson."

"Call me Hank, please, my dear."

That sounded a bit better, almost chivalrous.

"Can you turn on some lights, Mr. Carson? I can't see to take notes."

"Just walk straight ahead—you can't miss me."

She did just that and soon saw the dim outline of a couch and the perch of Mr. Rambo, who had been quiet up to this point. She saw a chair near the couch and sat down in it with a thud because it was lower than she expected it to be. Then she smelled liquor.

Resourceful reporter that she was, she pulled out a tiny pen-light from her purse and shined it on her notebook.

"Turn off that goddamn light!" yelled Carson. "It's hurting my eyes!"

Maxine kept it on and started to ask her first question. "Why did you get into the carnival . . ."

Carson leaped to his feet and was on top of her in seconds. "I said, turn off that goddamn light!"

Maxine screamed. "Get off me, you drunken skunk!" She tried to shove him off, but he held onto her so tightly that they both tumbled to the floor. This time, she was the one on top and was able to get to her feet. As she tried to get away from him, he grabbed her left leg and hung on. "Let go, you dirty bastard!" she yelled.

At that point, Mr. Rambo came to life and flew directly into Maxine's face. She ducked her head but could still feel his claws nicking her arms.

"DIRTY WHORE, DIRTY WHORE!" screamed the parrot.

Finally able to dislodge Carson's hands from her leg, Maxine crawled to the door. She beat on it and yelled, while the bird continued to make passes at her head and arms.

TOM

THE PHONE RANG just as I was sitting down to a dinner of left-over spaghetti.

"Hello."

"Tom, I need you."

"Maxine? What happened?" I could barely hear her. "Are you hurt?"

"Come to your friend's pastry shop." Then she hung up.

I grabbed my car keys and was out the door in seconds. It took me ten minutes to drive to Pirate Pastry. I parked in the rear of the shop and knocked on the door.

Morgan opened the door, a worried look on his face. "Come in, Tom."

"Is Maxine here?"

"Yeah, yeah." He stepped aside to allow me to enter and I ran to Maxine, who was sitting next to Kathy at one of the small tables. Kathy was dabbing at several bloody wounds on Maxine's arms.

"God, what happened to you? Are you okay?"

"Drink this," Kathy was saying to Maxine. "It's brandy, and it'll settle your nerves."

"Do you need stitches?" I asked, sitting down next to her and putting an arm around her shoulder.

"The wounds are not very deep," said Kathy. "They just sting when I put this salve on."

Maxine started to shiver, so I ran out to my car to grab a blanket I kept in the trunk. I ran back in and draped it over her shoulders. In the meantime, Dan had brewed some tea, and he handed a mug of it to her. She needed both hands to keep it steady as she drank. At first, she gulped it so fast that some trickled down her chin. I took the mug from her and held it so she could drink more slowly. She stopped shaking after a few more minutes and looked around at the three of us.

"Thanks, you guys. I'm sure glad you were here," she said to Dan and Kathy.

"Yeah, great," I said, "but why were you here? It's pretty late for you to be open."

"Wedding cakes," said Kathy. "We've got five to do in three days, so we had to stay late to get them started."

I turned to Maxine, finally getting the nerve to ask her what was going on. "So what happened?"

"I went in to interview Hank Carson, and he lunged at me for, I think, obvious reasons."

"Did he try to rape you?" I asked.

"Not sure he was capable of that in his condition. He was really drunk. Not sure he'd be capable of it anyway, if you get my meaning." She smiled feebly. "He's a little guy." She held up her hand and formed her thumb and forefinger into a very small configuration. I don't know if it was the relief that she wasn't

119

raped or the way she said it, but the tension finally faded away. We all laughed at what she said.

"And then?" I asked.

"The speed of his attack knocked us both out of my chair and onto the floor, and I wound up on top. When I tried to pull away, he held onto my leg and wouldn't let go. Then that goddamn parrot started screaming that I was a whore and then began to claw at my arms and peck at my head. That's how I got these wounds."

"How'd you get away?" asked Dan.

"The door was locked, but I kept beating on it and yelling as loudly as I could. At first, no one came because the park was full of people and there was a lot of noise. I fell down and, in the process, I guess I triggered some kind of latch because the door flew open. I fell outside and down the wooden steps."

"And what happened next?" asked Kathy, her eyes wide with anticipation.

"A clown came along and led me off to the side and gave me some water."

"Oh, so Father Eddie came to your rescue," I said.

"Father Eddie is really a clown?" said Dan, scratching his head. "He's not a defrocked priest?"

"It's a long story," I said.

"No, it wasn't Father Eddie," said Maxine, shaking her head. "It was the new clown who runs around made up to look like the devil."

"Now, I'm really confused," said Dan, shaking his head.

"He arrived yesterday to replace a clown who never showed up," said Maxine. "He told them he had laryngitis, so he points a lot. I've never heard him speak." She took a deep breath before continuing. "He gave me some water and led me along the side of the carnival grounds to the street. Then he pointed toward your shop and I staggered off, expecting him to follow. When I looked around, the street was empty."

Maxine took another sip of her brandy. "And here I am. That's all I know." She looked drained.

I had to ask her what might be a painful question. "What about your camera?"

Maxine started crying. "Actually it's Inez's camera. I ran out of film, so I started using hers. It's still in Carson's office, I guess, somewhere on the floor. Unless that bird pecked it into little pieces."

"Is everything on it still? I mean, all the images you've taken here? What about the ones from Inez that you kept from Bickford?"

"I'm afraid so," she said. We exchanged knowing glances about the images that had set Seth Barlow off on his murderous rampage.

"I've downloaded all the stuff from my Ecuador assignment and the other shots for this essay from my other cameras, so everything is not lost, but I need the shots from today to finish my essay. If I don't give the editors what they want, I won't get any more assignments."

"You mean, 'a parrot pecked my camera to smithereens' will not be an acceptable excuse?" said Dan, laughing.

"I'm afraid not," said Maxine, shaking her head. "These are tough times in national journalism, especially for anyone who tries to freelance."

I was amazed that her mind was still on her assignment. Anyone else would have given up a long time ago.

Maxine continued, "The attitude of the editors will be that there are plenty more hungry photogs out there, ready to pick up the pieces of my unfinished assignment. The editors wouldn't hesitate to give me the boot."

"And I thought the pastry business was brutal," said Dan, shaking his head.

"We've got to get that camera back," I said, even though I had no idea how to do that, "but Carson probably won't let us back on the Midway, and he's got enough goons to keep us away."

"Maybe Eddie could help us," Maxine said. "He's a decent guy."

"Except when he's around little choir boys," I said, rather unkindly.

"Maybe I can help," said Dan, "by putting on my mayor's hat. He can't keep me off the very land that I gave him permission to pitch his tents on. That's city property!"

"I'll go with you," I said. "I can nose around while you're distracting Carson and maybe talk to the good padre. We'll improvise when we get there."

"What about me? This is really my fight!" said Maxine, ruefully. "I need to go with . . ."

I put up my hand. "Think about it, Maxie. There's no way you can go near the place after what happened."

"Stay here with me for a while," said Kathy, "and then I'll drive you to your hotel. What you need more than anything is a long, hot shower and a good night's sleep."

TOM

WHEN DAN AND I PULLED UP IN FRONT of the carnival, the show was over for the day and people were walking out of the entrance. We got out of the car and moved in the opposite direction from the departing crowd.

"Just a minute, guys," said a voice. "We're closed for the day." It was Vinny, the beefy guard we met a few days ago. He stood in our path with his giant arms crossed.

Although the guard outweighed him by a hundred pounds or more, Dan stood toe-to-toe with him. "I'm the mayor of this town, and I want to speak to the boss. Take me to Hank Carson right now!"

As a big man who had probably used his size to intimidate people all his life, Vinny seemed taken aback that someone smaller would challenge him. "Mr. Carson's not available right now," he said. "He's . . . he's . . . gone to bed."

"Well, wake him up then," I shouted, gaining some bravado from Dan.

"Look, asshole, you need to come back tomorrow when we're open. *Comprende?*" He grabbed us by the arms and began to propel us out the entrance.

"It's okay, Vinny," said another voice. "I'll handle it." Father Eddie stepped out of the shadows at the perfect moment, as if he had been watching our little scene for a while.

"Good," I said. "I was going to ask for you next. Can we talk somewhere a bit more private?"

Father Eddie nodded.

As we walked, I reintroduced Eddie to Dan. We sat down on a picnic bench near a food cart before anyone said anything else.

"And where is the lovely Ms. March tonight?" asked Eddie.

I wasn't sure if he was putting me on or if he really didn't know what had happened to Maxine in his boss's clutches, so I said, "She's not here because your boss tried to rape her a few hours ago." Why not go for the jugular, I thought. Although Maxine hadn't been sure that Carson had rape in mind or was even capable of it, I figured the mention of it would get Eddie's attention.

Eddie started to laugh. "That's impossible," he said. "I left her with him in his office an hour or so ago for an interview." He looked around conspiratorially before continuing. "Besides, I happen to know that my good friend and benefactor Hank Carson is as impotent as a neutered cat."

"That doesn't mean he didn't try," I said. "He jumped on her and they fell on the floor, and that goddamn bird started pecking her arms and face."

Eddie looked genuinely surprised at our story. "I am really sorry," he said, "and appalled. Is she okay? Does she plan to press charges?"

"I doubt it, but she wants her camera back."

"Well, of course she does," he said, relief showing on his face. "Where is it?"

"In her mad scramble to get away from Carson, she left it in his office. It's still in there, I guess."

Eddie stood up. "Wait right here, and I'll just go in there and get it for you." He walked down the Midway toward Carson's large motor home/office.

"Well, that was easier than I thought," said Dan. "I'm glad I didn't have to get rough with that guy Vinny. I'd have hated to hurt him."

"Yeah, he needs to be able to continue to work here without nursing a broken arm or a bloody nose and black eye."

"Or two," said Dan, grinning.

"MY GOD, HELP ME! SOMEONE HELP ME!" Eddie was standing in the doorway of the office, looking inside.

We ran to him and stepped inside. Both Dan and I gasped at what we saw.

Hank Carson was sprawled face-up across the desk, his face a mass of blood. Mr. Rambo was next to him, his insides spilling out from his lifeless body.

125

TOM

ALTHOUGH WE WERE ALL IN SHOCK, I ran into the room after Eddie—not so much to help anyone but to see if I could find the camera. There was valuable information on it and, if the police took it as evidence, those photos would never see the light of day.

While Eddie was checking for a pulse—an idle effort, it was plain to see—and Dan helped him, I looked around. I quickly saw the camera under one of the chairs. With the two of them preoccupied, I was able to grab the camera and slide it into the pocket of my pants.

"God, there's even blood over here," I said, feigning an interest in checking out the scene of the crime. "The attack must have been pretty savage."

"What?" Eddie seemed in shock as he stood over his friend's body. Unfortunately, I had seen a few dead bodies in my lifetime and was much more accustomed to them than he was. I had almost forgotten how terrifying it was the first time.

"You'd better sit down," Dan said to Eddie. "I'm going to call the chief."

He glanced at me and I nodded. "Maybe I should step out-side," I said. "Maybe we should all step outside."

Both of us walked over to Eddie, helped him to his feet, and led him out the door and down the steps. A crowd of carnies had gathered and were whispering among themselves.

Marge Daniels, the fat lady, was the first to step forward. "Eddie, darlin', what's wrong?" She sat down beside him and all but smothered him in her arms.

"He's dead, Hank's dead," he murmured.

The crowd gasped at the news.

"What the hell happened in there?" shouted Ace St. Romaine, the sword-swallower. "Can anyone tell me?"

Dan stepped forward. "I'm Dan Morgan, the mayor of Taft-by-the-Bay. A terrible thing has happened. Your boss has been murdered."

More gasps from the crowd.

"Does anyone have a cell phone? I left mine in the car," Dan asked.

When no one responded, I took the opportunity to get Dan's keys and walk out the Midway to the car, as much to hide the camera as to get his cell phone. After I unlocked the car, I quickly shoved the camera under the seat and found Dan's phone in the center console. As I turned to walk back, I was aware of someone watching me from just inside the carnival grounds.

"God, you scared me!" I said to the clown with the devil face.

He bowed and gestured for me to follow him back to where the others were standing. Had he seen me stash the camera or, if he did, would he care? At this point, it didn't really matter.

I walked up to Dan and handed him the phone. Dan turned away from the others and talked briefly to whoever picked up.

"The police will be here right away," he told everyone, when he got off the phone. "Maybe you should all move back a bit to give the authorities some space."

They did as he said, and I stepped to the side where I could keep an eye on the car. I scanned the crowd for the devil-faced clown but did not see him. His creepy manner and his face made me shudder.

We milled around for at least ten minutes and then heard the sirens, first of an ambulance and then from four patrol cars, two from the city and one each from the county sheriff and the Oregon State Police. Dan stepped forward to greet who I assumed was the chief and he, in turn, introduced Dan to the others. The group huddled for a few minutes, then stepped up into the office.

Eddie had to move aside to let them in and he did so with the loyal Marge still trying to comfort him. By this time, her thin-man husband Monte was hovering nearby.

"You folks can go back to your trailers," said a young deputy, as he rolled out crime scene tape around the area in front of the motor home/office. The crowd moved back and then turned and walked away. I noticed that two tall state troopers were now in position at the entrance to the carnival grounds.

"I said you need to go home," said the deputy, when he realized that I wasn't moving.

"I came with the mayor," I said. "I don't work for the carnival."

"And you are? . . ."

"Tom Martindale. I live in Gleneden Beach, and I happened to come here tonight with Mayor Morgan."

"And that would be for what reason?"

"That's okay, Crawford, I'll handle this," said a voice from the doorway. The chief himself was standing in the doorway, and I could see Dan behind him. "Mr. Martin. Come on over here."

I complied.

"Dan tells me you were here with him tonight."

"Yes, sir, I was."

Law enforcement people always make me nervous although I've never had so much as a speeding ticket. Of course, I have had my share of scrapes in recent years, but none were my fault. I was even in jail once, but the charges were dropped and my record cleared. Despite all of this, I still feel myself start to grovel in their presence, as if anything I said that they didn't like would get me arrested.

"You came in here and saw the body?"

"Yes, Chief, I did." 'Chief' sounded less groveling than 'sir.' "We were behind Father Eddie and when he screamed, we followed him inside. It was a natural reaction, I think."

"Did you touch anything?"

"No, I did not. I think Dan may have touched the body to see if there was a pulse. I just watched them."

"Lots of blood. Did you step in any of it?"

"I don't think I did." I steadied myself as I raised one shoe and then the other to check the soles. "No, no blood on my shoes."

"Okay, great. Thank you." He turned to Dan, who had moved down the steps by this time and was standing next to me. "You gents can go," said the chief, "but stay close to the phone."

"Will do, Chief," said Dan, as he turned me around and pushed me toward the car.

"This is a nightmare," he whispered. "Let's get out of here. I need a drink."

As we got into the car, I noticed that the devil-faced clown had reappeared by the entrance. Like he had done before, he bowed toward me.

"That guy gives me the creeps," I said, as Dan started the car and turned it around.

"What guy, Tom?"

I pointed to where I had seen the clown, but no one was standing there.

TOM AND MAXINE

I KEPT AWAY FROM MAXINE for a day and a half, deciding that she needed to rest more than hang out with me. Kathy took food to her. With Carson murdered, the carnival closed. Yellow police tape surrounded the fairgrounds. Where excited parents with their kids in tow had once walked in anticipation of an evening of fun, darkened trailers and motor homes stood, their occupants—whether freaks or roustabouts—seldom came outdoors.

I didn't go near the place, but the police chief kept Dan informed about the investigation into Carson's death. Father Eddie seemed to have taken charge and was constantly asking the chief when the group could pack up and move on.

For his part, the chief was stymied in his investigation. His technicians had not found incriminating fingerprints in the office, nor had a weapon been located. The body of a middle-aged man had washed ashore ten miles north, but that seemed unrelated to Carson's death. It was so decomposed that his features were obscured. The chief had sent the fingerprints to the Oregon State Police Crime Lab, but results had not yet come back.

Two nights later, I asked Maxine out to dinner. We ate at one of my favorite Lincoln City restaurants, the Blackfish Café. After a period of small talk, I decided it was time to get serious.

"What are your plans?"

"I guess you'd like to get rid of me," she said, smiling weakly.

"Naw, not really. I'm getting used to having you nearby again."

"Well, that is a surprise. We haven't exactly been close for several years. I appreciate that you helped me carry out this assignment, but enough is enough. You've got your own life to live—I mean your professional life. Besides, I need to get back to New York to pick up what's left of my career. I really need to hustle up some work."

I looked around to make sure no one could hear us. "What are you going to do with those photos Inez took in Ecuador? Won't they be hard to sell? And what's the context? I mean, have you got hard facts to go with your images? Even if Barlow is a CIA agent, what does that prove if you don't have a story to go with those shots? And can you prove he is in the CIA?"

"You're right, as usual."

"I don't want to be right. I just want to help you figure out what to do."

"I appreciate that, Tom, more than you realize."

"Another thing that puzzles me is why you didn't print those photos right away—to see what she actually got."

"Easy to answer," she said. "Inez used a Leica."

"Like the one you used to have."

"Yes, and I used mine in Ecuador. Most of the time I prefer digital because it is much faster. In today's world, you've got to be fast. Inez was more old school; it was a point of pride for her to stick with the tried-and-true. It gave her photos a quality that harkened back to the 1930s, when photojournalism began. I think she felt that you can't rush quality. But that isn't always possible in today's world. Anyway, it means I have to get them processed in the old-fashioned way, and I'm not sure who I can trust."

"And speaking of those photos you and Inez took in Ecuador, have you figured out what to say to Paul when he realizes that you gave him the wrong camera?"

"I know, I know," she said, a sad look on her face. "He's always done so much for me I hated to double-cross him."

"Even for a journalistic scoop?"

She smiled. "Even for that."

"So, how can I help?"

"I would like to get back onto the carnival grounds and take some shots from a high point to give the overall feel of the place. Then I'd feel that my assignment was complete."

"Not the best idea you've ever had," I said. "There is a killer out there, or have you forgotten?"

"There is that," she said, frowning.

I paused for a moment as I considered how to reply. No question, I'd help her. If I didn't, she'd go without me. "I can see if Danny can get us back in."

"Yeah. Thank you, Tom."

"Would day or night be best?"

"Maybe at dusk, when the light is fading but still strong enough to help me capture the mood of the place," she said. "I mean, it's creepy enough in the daytime, but dusk would give my shots more pizzazz."

"Creepy pizzazz," I said, laughing. "My specialty. How about tomorrow, late afternoon?"

"Perfect. I'll pack my bags and be ready to leave right afterwards."

We drove back to the hotel, and I insisted on walking her to the door. She inserted the room card, pushed the door open, and stepped in.

"Oh my god, no," she yelled.

Maxine's room had been ransacked—the bed was overturned, the mattress cut open, and on the floor, all the drawers emptied, her bags slashed, and her notebooks torn up.

"God, a maniac is after me," she moaned, sinking into the only chair not on its side.

"Your cameras?"

She patted her oversized handbag. "I never leave home without them."

TOM AND MAXINE

IT WAS NEARLY DARK when we arrived at the carnival grounds that night. Even though the show was closed by police order, many of the lights were still on. I suppose the crew kept the generators going to provide lights for all the motor homes and trailers. It might also have been a safety concern, what with a killer still at large.

We walked along the east side, hiding in the grove of trees that abutted the grounds. We darted from tree to tree, but that soon seemed idiotic because no one was there to see us.

I stopped when we came to a gate with a chain and padlock closing it off. Up close, however, I saw that the lock hadn't been snapped so I easily removed it. I swung the gate open very slowly, hoping the loud squeak would be lost in the wind that had started to blow. Maxine and I ducked inside, and I pulled the gate closed again.

"Where do you want to go to take your shots?" I whispered.

"Up on that thing," she said, pointing to the Zipper. The ferocious ride sat straight ahead of us.

"How're you going to get up high enough to get a good vantage point?" I asked. "It's not moving."

She paused and turned to look me straight in the eyes. "I'm going to get on, and you're going to pull that lever. The machine will raise me up a bit, and then you'll stop the rotation. I'll take my shots, and you'll bring me back down."

"Not a good idea," I said. "You remember how nonmechanical I am. I can't even thread a needle to darn my socks."

"I've been watching the guys who run this thing for a few days, and all they do is pull the lever and the machine starts moving. The more you push it to the right, the faster it goes. You just need to barely nudge it."

As if to prove her point, Maxine stepped up onto the wooden platform at the front of the machine and pushed the lever. The Zipper came creaking to life, albeit very slowly.

"See," she said, smiling. "A piece of cake."

I moved toward her and stood in front of the lever. She was already opening the door on the lowest car and stepping into it. She pulled it closed, and I heard it snap shut.

"Don't take any chances, Maxie," I said. "Get your shots quickly so I can get you back down here."

She signaled that she was ready, and I pushed the lever. The Zipper started moving, and she was soon off the ground. I stopped it. She gave me a thumbs-down. Obviously, she was not high enough to get the images she wanted. I pushed the lever again and in a few seconds, she was higher and gave me a thumbs-up. I stopped the machine. She started taking shots in all directions, seemingly oblivious to the height or any danger.

Just then, someone pushed me hard from behind.

"I'll take over now, professor," a man hissed.

I fell face down and when I tried to get up, I felt a blow to my head. I also felt a needle going into my arm. The man turned from assaulting me and stepped in front of the control panel. It was the clown with the devil's mask.

Although I was dizzy, I was not unconscious, so I could watch his every move. I just couldn't to do anything about it— my arms and legs seemed paralyzed.

Maxine was still taking photos from high above, but as the clown turned up the speed, she became aware and looked down. When she saw the devil clown, she screamed. The Zipper began picking up speed and was about to go into its horizontal configuration, but then the clown stopped it abruptly, causing smoke to pour out of the ride on all sides and Maxine's car to start gyrating wildly.

Having stopped the Zipper, the clown started climbing up to where Maxine was. She forced open the door of the car she was in and got out, madly scrambling up the framework to get up to the next car. She managed to get into the other car, where she crouched in a corner, shielding the camera and trying to hold the door closed because the latch apparently did not work properly.

By this time, her screams had attracted the attention of the carnival crew, who came running out of their motor homes and trailers. Among them was Father Eddie, who recognized me and ran over.

"Are you all right, Tom?" he asked, helping me to my feet. I was still dazed and kept trying to shake off the effects of whatever the devil clown had drugged me with.

"Maxine's up there, and that clown with the devil face is trying to get to her," I managed to say.

Maxine's screams were growing louder.

"We've got to get her down, fast," I pleaded. "He'll kill her!" We looked up and the clown had reached the car Maxine was hiding in. Each time he grabbed for her camera bag, she pulled back, causing the little car she was in to rotate.

"Any of you guys know how to run this thing?" I yelled at the men standing nearby.

One stepped forward and looked at Eddie.

"Do it, Cliff."

With Eddie's consent, the man ran up to the control panel and pushed the lever hard to the right.

Just at that moment, the clown had been making a lunge at Maxine. The abrupt movement caused him to lose balance and he fell through the air, his billowing clown suit catching on one of the protruding struts of the Zipper. He dangled there for a moment, swaying back and forth, before falling the rest of the way to the ground where his head struck an iron tent peg.

Father Eddie and I ran over to him. The devil mask had slipped off, the garish red replaced by the real stuff oozing from the man's mouth.

"If I'm not mistaken, your new clown was a CIA agent," I said.

Eddie patted Tom on the arm. "You'd better sit down. You're not making any sense."

"Have you seen him before?" I asked him.

"Can't say I recognize him," said Eddie. "He was sent here a week ago by the company when Burt didn't show up. He told me he always kept the mask on to stay in character. We clowns are odd that way, so I didn't think anything of it."

"Anyone going to get me down from here?" yelled Maxine from high above.

Both Eddie and I looked up at her and exchanged glances of chagrin.

"Sorry, Maxie."

Cliff moved the lever and the Zipper began to descend slowly. Maxine was on the ground in seconds. I stepped forward to help her out of the still moving car. She was shaking, so I took off my coat and draped it over her shoulders. Eddie brought her a blanket. We led her to a nearby bench, and Eddie pulled a flask from his pocket.

"Drink this. It's brandy and it'll warm you up a bit."

She took a big gulp and asked, "Who is it? Seth Barlow?"

"Probably," I said. "No one knows what he looks like but you."

I helped her to her feet, and she walked over to where the clown was lying. She looked briefly at his face and turned away. "It's him," she said with a shudder. "God, what a fool I was to ever get involved with him."

I had figured that out a long time ago but didn't press the point with Maxine. It was, after all, none of my business who she became involved with.

"How could you know it would lead to this kind of thing?" I said, to be kind. I guess I really didn't care to know more. Her life was her life, and I had no part in it.

139

TOM, MAXINE, AND PAUL

Although I've been a big movie fan for many years, I have never lived my life as if parts of it were scenes from a film I liked. That being said, the setting at the Portland air base the following morning reminded me of the final scenes in *Casablanca*, that great World War II love story of misbegotten love in war-torn French Morocco.

Maxine and I had arrived from the coast about a half-hour before Paul Bickford's plane was due. As usual, he had worked his magic and his high-level government connections from wherever he was when I called him so that we were allowed to leave town.

Before we left the coast, we had walked to Pirate Bakery for coffee and scones. They weren't open, but Kathy and Dan were still working on the wedding cakes and were glad to see us. As we explained the whole sequence of events, I noticed a black SUV drive down the street toward the carnival grounds. Fifteen minutes later, the same vehicle returned and turned left onto Highway 101. I had no doubt that Bickford had arranged for Barlow's body to be removed. I also had little doubt that the whole incident would never be made public or even rate a tiny item in the local newspaper. He always worked that way, quietly and effectively.

Seth Barlow's name would never be inscribed on the CIA wall of heroes. I doubted that his work for that agency would even be acknowledged in the future. A rogue agent might as well be invisible after disgracing the agency. As to why he killed Hank Carson, we'll probably never know.

Maxine and I shared small talk while we waited. Did she have enough to complete her assignment? Yes, thanks to me. What would she do with Inez's images? She would give them to Paul after all, with apologies. Would she continue as a freelance photojournalist, despite the odds against success? She would keep at it for a while and maybe try for jobs in New York or Washington.

"Would you ever move back to a big city, Tom?"

"You mean New York?"

She nodded.

"No, I can't see that happening. Journalism as I know it has changed too much. I'm too old to learn new stuff, and I like my life here. Writing books is a lot more fun than writing magazine articles. And the pay, at least for me so far, is a lot better."

The whine of a small jet ended our conversation. The plane taxied over to where we stood. The engines stopped, the door swung open, and Maxine and I stepped forward.

An air force attendant got off first, then turned to help a little boy navigate the steep steps. The boy was dressed in a suit, dress shirt, and tie, as if he was going to church. He paused when he reached the ground and turned back toward to door. Paul

Bickford stepped off next, dressed in full camouflage, looking for all the world like the most powerful man on the planet.

Bickford leaned down and whispered something in the boy's ear, who turned to look at us. At my side, Maxine began to cry and ran toward them.

"Señora, señora," the boy cried, running to Maxine.

"Tito, you've come back to me!" She picked him up, and he kissed her. Putting the boy back on the ground, she turned to Paul, who had reached them at this point.

"Paul, how did you? . . ."

"You know I only answer questions on a need-to-know basis," he said, kissing her. The boy grasped them both by the legs and then the three of them walked back to the plane.

As per Claude Rains in *Casablanca*, left with no "usual suspects" to round up, I turned and walked back to my car. I doubt that any of them even glanced in my direction.

"The only thing necessary for the triumph of evil is for good men to do nothing."

—Edmund Burke

Five people with hoods over their heads are on their knees.
A man wearing cowboy boots with silver toes walks along in front
of each of them. He pulls off the hood of the first one—a young
Hispanic man—and shoots him between the eyes. He does the
same with the next man, also Hispanic. He nods to two thuggish-
looking men, and they pull the bodies to a nearby well and push
them in.

When he is standing in front of the last three, he pulls off
their hoods. Before him on their knees are a handsome Hispanic
man in his forties who has a black eye and bruises on his face, a
Hispanic woman in her thirties who would be attractive without
her heavy makeup and suggestive clothing, and a younger man
who looks like he has been badly beaten about the face and body.

The man steps back and cocks his gun.

146

BECAUSE OF HIS GOOD LOOKS, Lorenzo Madrid was often mistaken for the Spanish actor Antonio Banderas. His good friend and occasional client, Thomas Martindale, always teased him about this when they were together in public. At first, it embarrassed Lorenzo when both men and women slipped him their phone numbers written on the backs of business cards or once in a while a matchbook cover. Actually, they jotted the key information down on whatever writing surface was available.

The truth was that Lorenzo was not interested in becoming intimate with anyone, male or female. After his longtime lover, Scott, had been killed by a vicious gang many years before, he had thrown himself into his law practice. "I'm as celibate as a priest," he often told good friends.

Although he spent most of his time helping Mexicans out of their various difficulties, he took an occasional high-profile case. In this way, he earned substantial fees to enable him to take the bulk of his cases pro bono. For example, he once got Martindale out of jail when the woman he was accused of killing, Maxine March, turned out not to be dead.

Another time, he cleared the name of Martindale's cellist friend who was accused of terrorism. In the process, he had helped modify the more egregious provisions of the draconian Patriot Act passed in the hysteria following the terrorist attack on 9/11.

The publicity he got from winning that woman's freedom brought him several other high-profile civil liberty cases and a few corporate clients. In each instance, his dark, handsome looks helped sway juries, especially juries with a preponderance of women and gay men. For court appearances, he would exchange his usual blue work shirt and jeans for an expensive pinstriped suit, white shirt, and red tie. The white of the shirt contrasted with the brown of his skin. At certain key times during his presentations—where appropriate, of course—he flashed his white teeth, creating a different kind of contrast.

Lately, he had not had to don those big-city duds. Most weeks, he sat behind his well-worn desk and listened.

"*Señor* Lorenzo, if you could help me get papers for my son," said a tired-looking Hispanic man who was probably fifty but looked seventy. "I need his helping me in the fields."

"I can't just get him a green card that easily. It takes a long time. I assume he is illegal?"

The man looked frightened at the question.

"It's fine, *Señor* . . ." Lorenzo glanced at a piece of paper in front of him. "*Señor* Mendez. I am your attorney. I cannot reveal to anyone else anything you tell me inside this office. You can speak freely and not worry."

The man's shoulders sagged as if a burden had been lifted from them. "*Si, señor*. Diego slipped over the border like I did ten years ago. He is a good kid and worth any effort you can put to help him."

Later in the day . . .

"My Gloriana is a good girl," said a woman who had once been pretty but whose life had no doubt been burdened with constant trouble. She looked about to cry. "She just . . . you know, got in with the wrong crowd. She is going to have a baby now and has been takin' some drugs. Can you help her?"

"Has she seen a doctor? Is she healthy enough to be carrying a baby?"

The woman shook her head. "I don't know, *Señor* Lorenzo. She tell me nothin'. But I would not let her have an abortion, if that's what you're sayin'. I will raise the child myself."

"I was not suggesting abortion at all, *Señora* Bustamonte. I just wondered if she should see a doctor to make sure the baby is okay."

"Oh, pardon me, *señor*. I did not mean to insult you."

"Don't worry, *señora*. I am not that easily offended." Lorenzo handed her two cards. "This is the number of a free clinic here in Salem. Your daughter can go there for an examination to see how she is and how the baby is doing."

Señora Bustamonte nodded.

"The other card is for a drug clinic I work with. It is run by a former nun who helps young people like your daughter get clean. If you can get her to go there, maybe she can shake her habit before she is arrested and the state forces her to shake it—in jail."

"Oh, *dios mio*, jail. Not jail for my Gloriana." The woman began to sob.

Lorenzo walked over to comfort her but that only made her cry more loudly. In a few seconds she was wailing at the top of her lungs.

"You need to try to be strong for both of you . . . and the baby."

"The *niño*," she sobbed. "The poor *niño* to come into this kind of world."

At this point, the door to his office opened and his secretary, Dolores, stepped into the room, a worried look on her face.

149

"Lorenzo, is everything all right?"

Lorenzo looked both hapless and helpless. "It's *Señora* Bustamonte's daughter. She is worried about her. I have directed her to some places that might help her. Would you take her into the conference room and get her a cup of tea? Then, maybe you can help her make some calls."

Dolores Hidalgo, a stout, grandmotherly woman in her sixties, had been with Lorenzo since he opened his practice. She knew instantly what he wanted and how to carry out his wishes quickly. She whispered something to the woman in Spanish and helped her out of the room.

"You've got one more person out there to see you," Dolores called over her shoulder. "And a man who *says* he is your friend," she added somewhat hostilely.

"You know I have very few friends," said Lorenzo, laughing as he walked out into the waiting room.

"Tom! Good to see you, *amigo.*"

Tom Martindale sat thumbing through a magazine. "You need to put out some things for your visitors to read that are in English, Lorenzo."

"No, Tom. You need to learn Spanish," said Lorenzo.

They shook hands, and then Lorenzo noticed a young man sitting across the room whose clothing and attitude marked him instantly as a gangbanger.

"Hey! What about me?" the young man snarled. "You talk to a gringo before you will even look at me?"

Lorenzo walked over to the young man, who was wearing a cap turned backwards, a hoodie and white T-shirt, and drooping pants that looked like they could slide down his skinny frame at any moment. The tops of tattoos were visible on his neck—dragons that seemed to be creeping out of his shirt.

Lorenzo picked up a sheet of paper from Dolores's desk. "You must be Felix Zuño. Happy to meet you," he said, offering his hand.

The man looked surprised that Lorenzo had not taken up the challenge of his insult. After hesitating for a few seconds, he shook Lorenzo's hand.

"Come right in." Lorenzo said, opening his office door. Then he turned to Tom. "Lunch when I'm finished with Mr. Zuño?"

"Great. I'll take a walk around the block and be back in a while."

Lorenzo walked into his office, closed the door, and sat down behind his desk. He motioned for Felix to sit down in one of the chairs in front of it.

Felix commented, "You got lotsa' degrees on your wall over there. You must be as smart as everyone says you are. And good lookin' too. The little *chiquitas* must be crawlin' all over you. You know what I'm sayin'?"

Lorenzo straightened a yellow legal pad on his desk and picked up a pen. "Now, what brings you here, Mr. Zuño?"

"You can call me Felix."

"Okay then, it's a deal. Why did you come in to see me today, Felix?"

"I come here because guys you helped in the 'hood here, my best home boys, say you can help me get out of a gang up in Portland. Then maybe help me go back to school, and then, shit, maybe help me pass my GED and then go to college."

"What do you want to do, Felix? I mean, what kind of job would you train for?"

"Well, I dunno. A doctor maybe or a scientist."

"Are you good at science? Have you ever had biology or chemistry? Can you write well enough in English to sum up your findings . . ."

"Say what?"

"Findings. What you discover through scientific research in the lab. After you discover something new in the world of science, you need to write a report or an article to tell the world about it."

"Shit, man. I can just barely write my name, if you want to know the no-bullshit truth." Felix looked surprised at his own candor. "I never have said that before. Don't tell anyone."

Lorenzo smiled. "Your secrets are safe with me. I'm your attorney." He picked up the phone and punched in a number. "I'm calling a counselor who will arrange some tests for you to take, to see what your abilities are in science, social studies, writing, reading, and math—all the main areas on tests like for the GED. After we get those scores, come back and we'll see about getting you enrolled somewhere."

As Lorenzo spoke, Felix was nodding his head.

"Jim, hello. It's Lorenzo Madrid. Great. Fine. How are you? Listen, I'm sending over Felix Zuño for some testing. Maybe section 3."

Lorenzo and his counselor friend Jim Morris had worked out a code for ranking the abilities of people to be tested so as not to embarrass them. Section 3 equaled the third grade.

"Okay, good. This afternoon at three?" Lorenzo said and looked at Felix, who nodded. "He'll be there. And thanks as always, Jim."

Lorenzo handed Felix a card with the address and directions to the counseling center. "Give me a call when you have your test scores, and we'll take it from there."

By this time, Felix was no longer slouching and was even smiling. He shook hands with Lorenzo, and not the half-hearted shake of an hour ago but with a firm grip. "Sorry about the way I was before," he said, hanging his head. "I don't know why I act like that sometime."

"Don't worry about it, Felix. It's the gang member attitude. We'll get that straightened out eventually."

As Felix walked out the door, Dolores emerged from the conference room with the *señora* in tow.

"I think we've got things under control, Lorenzo. *Señora* Bustamonte is going to make some appointments at both clinics for her daughter. I will drive them there."

"That's great, Dolores," said Lorenzo. "You're fine with this, *señora*? Dolores is the person who picks up the pieces when I don't do my job very well."

"Thank you, both of you. I am so grateful. And my Gloriana will be too—but she doesn't know it yet."

The three of them laughed at that, and the *señora* departed. As she walked out the door, Martindale walked in.

"Good timing, Tom. Dolores, you remember my friend Tom Martindale."

Dolores, who was normally cordial and friendly, barely looked at Tom, who dropped his hand when she refused to shake it.

She ignored Tom and turned to Lorenzo. "I remember your friend very well. He has put your life in danger many times, and

I don't forgive him for that. You should stay away from him! I am going to take my lunch." Saying that, she turned, grabbed her coat and purse, and walked quickly out the door.

⊙ ⊙ ⊙ ⊙

"Dolores hates me," said Tom, putting down the menu at a nearby café. "Most people love me. I can't handle it when they don't."

"She is just being overly protective of me," said Lorenzo. "She thinks she's my mother. I guess maybe she is at times. I really don't have anyone who falls into that category."

A waiter took their order and walked away.

"Neither do I," said Tom.

"Maybe I fall into that category," said Lorenzo. "Who else tries to keep you from getting into trouble, Tom? You're the one with the tendency to take chances. So, what brings you to Salem?"

"I'm still keeping my distance from the university," he said. "That brief time there during last spring term was enough to make me realize that I've been out of the classroom too long to go back. All the texting and tweeting and downright rudeness by the students—I don't need that. So I've gone back on leave. I'll just teach every once in a while to keep my retirement fund active."

"Must be nice to have another income so you don't have to teach full-time," said Lorenzo.

"It's my book royalties—from that drug book. It's in a tenth printing, and it's been optioned by a producer down in Hollywood. It looks like a movie will be made. And I want you to play me."

Both started laughing.

"I need someone who brings on swoons," said Tom.

"I'm not feeling very swoon-worthy right now. All of these charity cases are getting me down," said Lorenzo.

The waiter returned with their soup and sandwich orders, and they began to eat.

"I thought you loved helping out your 'people,' as you so often call them," said Tom.

"I do get satisfaction from that, most of the time, but it often feels like I'm shoveling you-know-what against the tide," said Lorenzo. "The more I help the people who come through my door, the more of them with similar problems show up. I helped their friend or their sister or their brother, so I can help them. At least that's what they think. A lot of the time they are in a mess because of their own stupidity. It gets to me. I'm an attorney, not a miracle worker. And don't get me started about the chance of ever getting paid."

Lorenzo continued to eat his lunch, and Tom said nothing.

"But I told you all about this weeks ago on the phone," Lorenzo finally said.

"Yes, you did, but we agreed to talk about it some more in person, so here I am," said Tom, "here to cheer you up."

"I remember," said Lorenzo. He gazed into space for a moment and took a drink of water, then continued. "I am feeling a bit better now." He paused as if trying to decide what else to say. "But I really don't want to talk about it until I sort some things out. Personal stuff I can't even talk to you about."

"Okay," said Tom, shrugging his shoulders. "You know I'm always here for you."

Lorenzo nodded. "I know, and thanks. But enough about me. You obviously have something else on your mind besides trying to cheer up a tired, old attorney."

Tom looked around the café and lowered his voice. "It's nothing like getting me out of jail again and saving my career. You've done that already."

"Thank God for small favors," chuckled Lorenzo.

"All I want is to ask if you know anything about a seminary east of here being involved in laundering drug money."

Lorenzo shook his head as he finished his sandwich and asked, "That would be St. Gregory?"

"Yeah, I think that's the one."

"Haven't heard anything at all. I was hired by the diocese last year to defend a priest from there against charges that he molested some altar boys. I got him off because the boys' testimony was only circumstantial evidence that wouldn't hold up in court. He was reassigned to an out-of-state parish. I didn't set foot in the place. What have you heard?"

"Just a rumor from a source who helped me with my cocaine book. I thought I might do another book or an article focusing on the seminary as an example of how the drug cartels cover their tracks."

"I don't know what to tell you, Tom. I have no connections there and haven't heard anything through the grapevine."

"I understand. Just thought I'd ask. I really don't have any time to look into this myself. I need to get away. Maxine March came back into my life and right out again."

"The woman you were arrested for killing?"

Tom nodded.

"Tell me more," he said.

Tom spent the next half-hour telling Lorenzo about the carnival and the demented clown and about his and Maxine's brush with death.

"That's pretty extreme, even for you," Lorenzo said, shaking his head. "And then she goes off with that spooky army guy."

"Yeah, it's all true. So there's still no future for Maxine and me," Tom said, shaking his head and then changing the subject. "Well, I'm off on a book tour in Europe next week. But if you hear anything about this drug stuff, drop me an email. I might follow-up on it when I get back."

The waiter walked over with the bill. Both grabbed for it.

"I'll get it, Lorenzo. I invited you."

"Okay, Tom, I'll let you. I'm walking away from here with all of my fingers and toes for a change. That doesn't usually happen when you call me up and ask for my help. Safe travels."

Two weeks later, Madrid was sitting at his desk working on a brief when the door burst open and a woman barged in, trailed by a perturbed Dolores.

"I'm sorry, Lorenzo. I tried to stop her, but she just pushed me aside and rushed through your door."

"Don't worry, Dolores. I'm happy to take care of Miss . . ."

The woman folded her arms in defiance. "Oh, you are the smooth one, aren't you," she said as she settled herself in a chair opposite Lorenzo. She looked like she was in her forties, and she might have been pretty once, but now she looked tired, with dark circles under her eyes despite the heavy makeup. Her clothes were cheaply made and fairly scanty—short skirt and tight top that revealed more than anyone but a prostitute would want revealed.

Lorenzo sat staring at her, his hands folded on his desk. "You have me at a disadvantage, *señorita*. What is your name and what brings you to my office?"

The woman smoothed her skirt and ran a hand through her dyed red hair. She had calmed down a bit. "You don't remember me, do you?"

"No, I'm afraid we've never met, although I do see a lot of people here. Have you been here before with a legal problem?"

The woman suddenly got angry again, her face reddened. "I can't believe you don't remember me. My name is Consuelo Cortez. My friends call me Connie, but you can call me Miss Cortez! My brother is Gustavo Cortez, who we call Gus." She started to cry. "Do you even remember him? Like from court? You defended that lowlife priest from the seminary, Father Gordon. He's the one who molested all those little altar boys for years and years."

Lorenzo did remember the case but chose not to interrupt Consuelo's story.

"One of them was my baby brother Gus. An innocent if there ever was one. You were so high and mighty in court, with your fancy suit and your expensive ties and your shirts with cuff links. I hadn't ever seen cuff links before I saw yours. I bet the diocese paid you mucho dinero to get that pedophile off!"

"I guess you don't want to hear that I sometimes take high-profile cases where I get paid a lot of money, which I use here in the barrio to help people who can't pay me," said Lorenzo, a sad look on his face. "We call that pro bono."

"You got that right! I don't want to hear it! I don't care what you call it, but I say it is selling out your own people."

"I know how it looks, but I had my reasons. There was only circumstantial evidence against Father Gordon. I know the boys got roughed up a bit in court, but . . ."

"Roughed up! You crucified them, my brother included. They were innocent babies, and you made them look like they enjoyed what he did to them. You made them look like child prostitutes! You took the church's blood money . . ."

"You know, Miss Cortez, I really think I'm through sitting here and taking these accusations from you. Tell me what you want, or I'll have to ask you to leave."

Connie started sobbing, the tears quickly making her heavy mascara run down her face like a clown standing in the rain.

"I'm afraid tears won't work with me," Lorenzo said.

Connie stood up and held out her hand to stop him. "I don't want you to say another word until I finish what I came in here to tell you. Father Gordon was murdered a few days ago, and Gus has been arrested and accused of killing him. My innocent, twenty-year-old baby brother is in jail, and it's all your fault! If anything happens to him in there, his blood will be on your hands!" Connie fell to her knees, sobbing.

Lorenzo walked over to her and knelt down to comfort her, but she pushed him away.

ALL JAILS ARE GRIM, even if they are not old and falling apart. Lorenzo had been in a lot of them over the years, while meeting with clients. He was always struck by both the smells—disinfectant mixed with human sweat and urine—and the sounds— loud clanging of doors, shouts of men to one another across the cellblocks, shoes stomping along corridors as inmates lined up for food.

He and Connie had to pass through a series of double doors to get to the visitors' room, which was divided into cubicles— visitors on one side, inmates on the other. They sat down at the last one on the far end.

Lorenzo was dressed in his big-city attorney garb—grey suit, white shirt, and red tie. This was not the place for his blue work shirt and jeans attire. Connie had tried, without total success, to dress down. She wore less makeup than usual, but her skirt was still too short and her blouse—three buttons undone—a bit too revealing. Lorenzo hid a smile at her shoes—silver with some kind of blue spangles on the toes and encased in the heels, which were so high that she teetered back and forth when she walked.

"See what you did to my brother," Connie hissed, as she looked around.

Before Lorenzo could answer, a door at the other end opened and two beefy guards, both with shaved heads and scowls on their faces, led a small figure into the room and to the cubicle. Gus was wearing handcuffs and leg chains, both attached to a wide belt around the waist of his oversized yellow prison jumpsuit. He had black hair, sad brown eyes, and skin slightly lighter than his sister's, and he looked younger than his years, more like fifteen than twenty. Gus slumped wearily into the chair, his chains clanking.

"What happened to your face?" asked Connie.

"I . . . fell . . . in the shower. I guess I'm kind of clumsy now."

"Fell, my ass! Somebody's been messing with you. I'm not surprised. You're as pretty as a girl. Those perverts inside here would like to get a piece of you, no doubt."

She started to stand up like she was going to walk over to a guard and complain. Lorenzo grabbed her arm and shook his head. She sat down.

"Not now. I'll take care of it later," he told her.

"Yeah, you'll take care of it," said Connie, scoffing. "I won't hold my breath."

"Connie," said Gus. "It's okay. I'm learning to cope. This big black guy is helping me. He watches my back in the yard."

"Yeah, I'll bet he does. Watches your back and your ass."

"No, he's a good guy. He's older than most of the guys in here. He says I remind him of his grandson. I'm teaching him how to read."

Gus turned to Lorenzo and reached over to shake his hand.

"No touching!" yelled a guard.

Gus pulled back his hand. "It's nice to meet you," he said to Lorenzo. "Thank you for coming. I've read about how you do a lot for your people . . . my people."

"I try my best."

"Yeah, you try your best for those with the big bucks, like the diocese," interrupted Connie. "You tried a bit too hard for them, and the result is what you see before you—my baby brother in chains, disgraced, hurt, and in danger. His life is ruined because of you."

"Connie, stop! Mr. Madrid was only doing his job. I got caught up in something that was way over my head," he said, then turned toward Lorenzo. "I've never been lucky in my life. I've wanted to do bigger things than I'll ever get the chance to do now."

"Yeah," whispered Connie, motioning toward Lorenzo, "because of this guy."

"Quit it! I'm going to ask them to take me back to my cell if you don't stop criticizing Mr. Madrid."

Connie shrugged her shoulders and glared at Lorenzo.

"Tell me what happened the night Father Gordon was killed," said Lorenzo.

"I volunteer in the soup kitchen in the seminary where Father Gordon used to teach," said Gus. "I used to do it when I was in high school, and I started doing it again a few months ago, to help me forget what happened to me there."

"You mean when Father Gordon molested you?" asked Lorenzo.

Gus looked down and wiped away a tear. "Yeah."

"Why would you go back to a place with such bad memories, where you were abused?"

"After the trial . . ."

"Where you-know-who defended him," said Connie, pointing a thumb in Lorenzo's direction.

Gus ignored her and continued. "After the trial, Father Gordon was sent away to another state. For me, that was a big relief so I decided to go back to the seminary, I guess to get rid of my demons. I started going there a few nights a week after my classes at the community college. Things went well for a few weeks. Then, one night I was serving food to some of the homeless people who come there, and Father Gordon walked into the room like a conquering hero and started going from table to table, being greeted by the people who knew him. I couldn't believe my eyes! When he saw me, he got this smirk on his face, like he was saying,saying that he won and I lost."

"I can't believe the church let that beast come back!" said Connie. "Those innocent children suffered for nothing. He did not get punished, and he even got his old place back. Unbelievable!"

"What happened after that?" asked Lorenzo.

"His body was found in his cottage, a couple of hours after we cleaned up and I went home."

"Why did they arrest you?"

"I guess because someone saw me with him earlier," said Gus, hanging his head. "I walked out after him so I could talk to him. At first, I didn't see where he had gone, but then I saw him with one of the other guys, heading toward his cottage. I ran after him and called his name."

"And what did he do?"

"He had his arm around this other kid, and he stopped and turned around. I told him to leave the kid alone, and he just laughed. I started shouting, but he ignored me and led the kid into his cottage."

"What happened then?" asked Lorenzo.

"I gave up and walked to the bus stop and went home. That night, the cops woke me up banging on the door. When

I opened it, they pulled their guns and ordered me to get down on the floor."

"See what you caused here, Madrid!"

"Will you just quit that, Connie! Mr. Madrid had nothing to do with any of this."

"What happened to the other kid?" asked Lorenzo. "I wonder why he wasn't picked up too."

"Beats me. I guess he left the cottage after he and Father Gordon had sex or whatever they did together."

Lorenzo didn't say anything for a long time. He thought about what he had said to his friend Tom Martindale about being tired of doing legal work for people who could not pay and whose situations were hopeless. And then he thought about what his favorite law professor at UCLA had said to him long ago: "You must be true to those who need your legal help, no matter how poor they are or how hopeless their cases might be."

"Madrid, are you in some kind of trance?" asked Connie, breaking into his thoughts.

"Sorry, I was wondering if I had the time to take on another case."

"Yeah, especially since we can't pay you," sneered Connie.

Both Gus and Lorenzo ignored her this time, her outbursts were now so predictable.

Lorenzo was quiet for several more minutes, and then said, "I'll take your case."

"Now, you're talkin'," said Connie.

"But Connie's right, I have no money to pay you," said Gus. "I'm broke."

"I'm not doing this for the money," said Lorenzo, glaring at Connie. "Contrary to what your sister believes, I do this kind of case for free to serve justice. The cases she's always talking about, where I do get the big bucks, are why I can afford to do this."

Connie squirmed in her chair but, for a change, said nothing.

"Let me try to get you moved to a safer place in the jail. The sheriff owes me a favor or two. I'll be back to see you in the morning so we can go over the facts again. I need to prepare for the hearing to determine if they have enough to hold you for trial."

"Visiting hours are over!" shouted the guard. "You must leave immediately."

Gus got up and turned, his chains rattling as he walked to the door between the two guards.

Connie got to her feet and adjusted her blouse and skirt, which she pulled down slightly as they passed the guard by the door.

THE COURTROOM WAS NOT AS MAJESTIC LOOKING as some others in the state where Lorenzo had appeared. No polished oak railings and antique furniture, no high ceilings with fans slowly turning and light fixtures that had once been gaslights. This courtroom was plain and drab and rather drafty.

As soon as he entered the room, Lorenzo noticed that the audience was filled with priests and nuns—no doubt they were there as a sign of devotion to the dead priest. A stout Hispanic lady sat in the back, and a young Hispanic man, who looked a lot like Gus, was sitting next to her. Next to him was someone who had to be a gangbanger or former gangbanger. His shaved head and tattoos and low-slung pants gave him away, as did a deep scar on his face. Behind them sat several older Hispanic men wearing expensive-looking suits and cowboy boots with silver caps on the toes.

The prosecution team was already seated when Lorenzo walked in. The team was headed by a tall, thin man with wire-rimmed glasses that covered what Lorenzo immediately thought of as "mean eyes"—the D.A. himself. Next to him sat a short, stout woman wearing a dress that was too tight to cover her ample figure without bulges appearing here and there—the second seat. And seated slightly apart from them, a young man was constantly arranging and rearranging files so voluminous it seemed that they could topple to the floor at any time. He was sweating despite the coolness of the room—the go-for.

Connie sat in a chair just behind the rail that separated the audience from the attorney tables and the judge's high bench. Lorenzo nodded to her but did not walk over to talk to her. Better to keep her off the radar for now.

All eyes turned toward the door as the same thuggish-looking guards led Gus into the courtroom. Lorenzo had bought him a suit that made him look more like a choirboy than a murderer. He looked like he had been beaten up again—with a black eye and bruises on his face.

"I'm sorry I couldn't get you transferred," whispered Lorenzo to Gus after he was seated next to him. "You're having a hard time, I know."

"That's okay, Mr. Madrid. Hey, I want to thank you for the suit. You know, I've never had a suit before. Even for church. We couldn't afford it."

"You're welcome. You look good, except for your face. I decided I wouldn't try to cover up your bruises so the judge could see them. It says a lot about you and what you're going through."

Then the court clerk spoke. "All rise. Superior Court of Marion County is now in session, the Honorable Ian McKinney presiding."

Lorenzo noticed that the judge nodded to the people at the prosecution table and to some of the spectators.

"A Catholic judge. The deck may be stacked against us," he whispered to himself.

"What did you say?" asked Gus.

"Just muttering to myself like I always do before a trial. Don't worry."

The clerk then detailed the reason they had assembled: a preliminary hearing to determine if Gustavo Cortez should be held for trial for the murder of Father Andrew Gordon.

The judge then called on the D.A. to state the case against Gus and also to talk about the dead priest. It seemed to Lorenzo that he was allowed to talk too long about Gordon, even showing photos of him doing various good works in the church and the community. As he did so, his supporters in the audience nodded their approval.

"And most exemplary of all," said the D.A. in closing, "was his fine work with the young men of the parish."

"Objection," said Lorenzo. "Facts not in evidence. This man, Father Gordon, was thrown out of this parish for what he did to these young men. I would hardly call it" . . . Lorenzo held up his hands to form quotation marks with his fingers . . . "fine work."

"Overruled," said the judge. "I will not allow a man of God to be disparaged in my courtroom."

"Your Honor," replied Lorenzo, "to hear the D.A. talk about Father Gordon, one would think he is being considered for sainthood."

"Mr. Madrid, you are walking very close to the line here," said the judge. "I do not want to have to hold you in contempt of this court."

"My apologies, Your Honor."

"The prosecution rests, Your Honor," said the D.A. "We see no reason that the young Mr. Cortez should not be held over for trial for the murder of Father Andrew Gordon."

Lorenzo shook his head but said nothing.

"Very well then, we will proceed with the defense. Are you ready to call your first witness, Mr. Madrid?"

"Yes, Your Honor," said Lorenzo, turning to look at the D.A. "However, I feel a bit at a loss here because of the overwhelming nature of the testimony about Father Gordon. Nowhere did I hear about any evidence that my client killed him."

"Well," said the D.A., sputtering slightly, "the police caught him red-handed."

"Funny, but I didn't hear testimony by even one police officer about how they connected the murder to my client. Who tipped them off so that they would even know about my client? Nor did we hear from anyone else who saw my client near Father Gordon on the night in question. It all seems very odd to me. I move that my client be released from custody for lack of evidence."

There were shouts from the audience of "No!" but the judge did not bang his gavel to quiet them.

"Mr. Madrid, you really don't expect me to rule in your favor, do you?"

"I guess not, Your Honor, but I had to try," said Lorenzo, as he walked behind Gus and put his hands on his shoulders. "This is not a cold-blooded killer. This is a young man who is a striver, a young man trying to improve his life. He has a desire to get an education and make something of himself. He wants to have a career and a family. Why would he derail all of that by killing someone?"

Lorenzo walked around the table and faced the judge. He talked about fifteen-year-old Gus going to work to support his family and the fact that he got good grades in school, "despite the lack of any role models or encouragement from anyone."

Lorenzo then turned and faced the audience. "I call Consuelo Cortez."

All eyes were on Connie as she walked to the witness stand. Lorenzo opened the gate and she stepped through it. Despite her attempt to tone down her appearance—wearing light makeup, hair in a bun, horn-rimmed glasses, no earrings, and loose-fitting clothing with no cleavage showing—Connie still looked like the prostitute that she was. Her shoes—covered in rhinestones with very high heels—gave her away. The heels were as high as the ones she had worn to the jail and, once again, Connie wobbled when she walked in them. Men sat stunned with their mouths open; the nuns looked horrified.

"State your name and your relationship with the defendant."

"Consuelo Cortez, but my friends call me Connie. Gustavo—we call him Gus—is my baby brother."

"Please tell us about Gustavo."

"Objection, Your Honor," said the D.A. "We should not waste the court's time with a lengthy biography."

"Sustained. Please be more specific with your questions, Mr. Madrid."

"Yes, Your Honor, I will try. Miss Cortez, you said Gustavo is your baby brother. How much younger is he?"

"Well, let's just say a few years," said Connie, pulling out her compact to check her makeup.

"Miss Cortez, you must refrain from powdering your nose on the stand," said the judge, sternly.

"Sorry, Judge, but I was afraid it was too shiny. I always try to look my best."

"I'm sure you do, but we need to stay focused this morning. Mr. Madrid, please advise your witness that she must refrain from these outbursts."

"Outbursts!" shouted Connie. "My brother is fighting for his life, and you talk about outbursts!"

"You are walking a fine line here, Miss Cortez," said the judge, pounding his gavel. "Do you know what contempt of court is?"

"Well, no, not really," said Connie, hanging her head.

"I am sure Mr. Madrid will tell you that it is not pleasant. I am sure you would not find it at all to your liking, although I am sure that some of our inmates would love to have you in their midst, but I can't allow that, now can I?"

"No, sir. I am sorry."

Lorenzo ignored what the judge said and the smattering of laughter from the spectators. "Miss Cortez, you must answer my questions to the best of your knowledge with no detours. Is that understood?"

Connie nodded her head.

"You were about to tell us the age difference between Gustavo and you."

"He is ten years younger than me."

"Was there a period when you cared for Gustavo?"

"Oh yes, I love him very much," she said, glancing at Gus.

"Your Honor, can the plaintiff's attorney please keep his witness in line?" said the D.A.

The judge stared at Lorenzo, but said nothing.

"*Care for* as in *take care of*," Lorenzo explained.

"Oh, I get it. You mean did I babysit him? Sure, all the time. Maybe most of the time."

"Were your parents there to take care of Gustavo too?"

"Well, er . . . um . . . they didn't . . ." Connie seemed reluctant to answer.

"Were they good parents?"

Connie hesitated, then squared her shoulders as if fortifying herself before she replied. "They were terrible parents. My father ran off with a girl younger than me, and my mother was a" . . . glancing at the judge . . . "whore."

"Objection, Your Honor!" said the D.A. "Miss Cortez's mother is not on trial here. She is not here to defend herself."

"That would be pretty hard, Mr. D.A. My mama has been dead for ten years. She died of a drug overdose. The guy she was in bed with was young enough to be her son, and he was a bad dude. I remember the night . . ."

"Objection, Your Honor! We do not need a case history of Miss Cortez's mother. I myself had alcoholics in my family."

"Well, la te da," said Connie, mockingly. "I am sure it was very tough for you growing up."

The judge's face turned red. "Mr. Madrid, you will control your witness, or I will have both of you removed from my courtroom. Is that clear?"

Lorenzo was embarrassed but noted that even some of the priests and nuns were trying to hide smiles.

"My apologies once again, Your Honor. This will not happen again. Correct, Miss Cortez?"

Connie nodded.

"Miss Cortez, does that mean that you raised Gustavo?"

"Yes, I did. From the time he was three or four. He was a good little kid so it was easy. I made sure he ate regular and had clean clothes and played with the right kind of kids. I made sure he went to school where he did very well."

"Was there a time when you turned to the church for help?"

"Yes, I felt it was important that he have the Catholic Church to fall back on. I mean, with such a chaotic family life, with our mother like she was and no father around. I have not had much education, so I wanted him to learn as much as he could so he could succeed in this world." Connie glanced at Gustavo and smiled, a look of pride on her face.

"Objection, Your Honor. I don't think we need to hear about Miss Cortez's thoughts on the value of education," said the D.A.

"I'll allow this line of questioning. Proceed, Mr. Madrid."

"Thank you, Your Honor. So you sent Gustavo to the seminary school for his education?"

"Yes, I did. He went through all the lower grades and high school there. We got to know Father Gordon and the monsignor and the other teachers pretty well. They got him scholarships so it did not cost me a dime. It was wonderful."

"Did there come a time when things became, to use your word, not so 'wonderful'?"

"I caution you here, Counselor, about where this might be leading," said the judge. "You may answer, Miss Cortez."

"You bet your ass. I found out that Father Gordon was balling my little brother and a lot of the other kids. I found out that Father Gordon was the biggest pervert you've ever heard of!"

The courtroom erupted in gasps of disbelief and angry shouts of objection from the D.A. The judge banged his gavel so hard that Lorenzo thought he had cracked the wooden surface of his desk.

"Order, order! I will have the bailiff clear this courtroom if this disturbance persists. Mr. District Attorney, do you wish to cross-examine this witness? Mr. Madrid is finished."

"Yes, Your Honor, I do," said the D.A., while looking at some papers on the desk. "Miss Cortez, where were you on the night of February 14, 2009?"

Connie smirked and said, "Maybe being someone's valentine."

There were groans from the spectators. Lorenzo shook his head, Gus buried his head in his hands, and the judge looked very angry.

"Do you take this proceeding seriously, Miss Cortez? I can assure you that the charges your brother is facing are no laughing matter. Answer the question, or I will hold you in contempt of this court and levy some pretty heavy fines against Mr. Madrid."

"Sorry, Judge, I got carried away."

"The answer to my question?" asked the D.A.

"Honey, I can barely remember what happened last week, let alone what happened three years ago."

The D.A. persisted: "July 17, same year? January 2010? April of last year?"

"Help my sister!" whispered Gus to Lorenzo. "Get her off the stand, please!"

"Objection, Your Honor," said Lorenzo. "The district attorney is badgering my witness by continuing to ask her questions she has said she does not know the answer to."

"I presume there is a point to all these dates," said the judge to the D.A.

"Yes, Your Honor, there is."

"Then I suggest you get to it and not waste any more of the court's time."

"Very well, Your Honor. I was laying the foundation for my next question."

The judge waved his hand and said, "I think we have enough of a foundation to build a skyscraper on."

"That's a good one, Judge," said Connie, a big smile on her face. "You're pretty funny when you want to be."

The judge glared at her but said nothing.

"Miss Cortez, these records here before me indicate that you were arrested for soliciting men to engage in unlawful prostitution on those dates."

There were gasps from the audience.

"Order, order," shouted the judge, this time without using his gavel.

Lorenzo jumped to his feet. "Objection. I fail to see the point of bringing up details of Miss Cortez's life. She is not on trial here. If anything, this shows her willingness to help her brother despite her own problem-filled life."

"Help him!" scoffed the D.A. "By teaching him how to be a pimp!"

Gustavo rose from his chair, his chains rattling. "Leave my sister alone!"

"Mr. Madrid, if you can't control your client, I will have him gagged. I will not tolerate such outbursts in my courtroom. The cells in our jail here will soon be filled with you and your entourage."

Lorenzo leaned down and whispered in Gus's ear. "I know it's bad, but you can't yell out like that. It'll only make it worse for you." He looked up at the judge. "I am sorry, Your Honor. It won't happen again. As I am sure you realize, my client is under a great deal of stress."

"I will take your word on that, Counselor. Proceed, Mr. D.A. It is almost time to adjourn for lunch."

"There is a question in the air, Miss Cortez. Your whereabouts on the dates in question?"

Connie sighed, then said, "Yeah, I was picked up, trying to make a buck. To tell you the truth, I can't remember the exact dates."

"Were there other times?"

"Objection, Your Honor," said Lorenzo. "Asked and answered."

"You have made your point, Mr. D.A. Anything else?"

"No, I am finished with this witness."

"Mr. Madrid, do you have any follow-up?"

"No, Your Honor, I do not."

"Very well, then, we stand adjourned until 2 p.m.," said the judge.

The clerk shouted "All rise," and the judge walked off through a side door. The spectators walked out of the courtroom. Lorenzo reached over and patted Gus on the arm before the guards led him away. Connie sat quietly sobbing in her seat.

⊙ ⊙ ⊙ ⊙

After lunch, with everyone in place once again, the judge said, "Anything else, Mr. D.A.?"

"No, Your Honor, the State rests," said the D.A. "We feel there is overwhelming evidence to hold Gustavo Cortez over for trial for the murder of Father Andrew Gordon."

"I agree," said the judge. "Do you have anything to add, Mr. Madrid?"

Lorenzo stood up and shouted, "You agree? Just like that?"

"Mr. Madrid, I have cautioned you repeatedly about raising your voice and disturbing my courtroom. I know you are trying

177

to help your client, but you must abide by the rules of procedure. And I set the rules of procedure in my courtroom."

"Do your rules include fairness and true justice? Do they include sitting by while a real railroad job is going on, a travesty of justice?"

"Mr. Madrid!" shouted the judge, pounding his gavel.

Lorenzo continued, "You would not allow me to discuss the fact that the sainted Father Gordon was a pedophile! He lured young boys into his lair and molested them. Any one of them could have killed him, but you won't allow me to introduce any testimony about that possibility. He ruined Gus Cortez. He ruined many others."

Lorenzo ignored the shouts from the judge and walked toward the railing that separated the bench area from the spectator seats. He pointed to a young man who had been in court all day. "I am sure he ruined this young man's life, as well as Gus's. I am sure he can testify as to what happened to him and many others. I'll bet he was there. Church officials have prevailed upon him not to testify and probably forced him to come here to sit with all these other Catholics in support of this monster, Father Gordon. But you have not allowed me to subpoena him or anyone else."

The judge had had enough. He pounded his gavel and shouted, "Bailiff, arrest this man and escort him from my courtroom."

The courtroom erupted once again; people were shouting at Lorenzo and trying to hit him as the two bullet-headed guards pushed him down the aisle. Connie was screaming and Gus was crying, slumped in his chair and looking more frightened than ever.

◉ ◉ ◉ ◉

That night, Lorenzo was sitting in the back of a crowded and dirty cell in the county jail. He was waiting to be released, having called another lawyer who arranged for payment of the fines the judge had levied against him.

Two men, one black and one white, walked up to him and pulled him to his feet.

"You are too good to be true," said the white one. "Nice and brown with smooth skin and an ass to die for, I'll bet."

"I don't think so!" said Lorenzo, as he lunged for the man, hitting him in the jaw.

But he didn't see the black man rush in from the side and punch him so hard in the groin that he collapsed and fell to the floor, seeing stars and then passing out.

◉ ◉ ◉ ◉

In the middle of that night, Gustavo Cortez sat in the isolation cell the sheriff had put him in for his own protection from the predators in the jail.

Despite many attempts to get a grip on his emotions, he had been unable to stop crying since he had been brought back from the courthouse. He thought about his plight: a long trial in which his sister would have to testify, few witnesses to vouch for his character, and no witnesses to place him anywhere but near Father Gordon before he was killed. The more he sat on his cot and thought about his certain conviction and what would follow—years and years of prison life where he would become a sexual prize—the more he cried. A future that might have been promising, or at least somewhat useful, was now nothing but a bleak tunnel he would never emerge from.

At a quarter to four, Gustavo Cortez pulled out a razor blade he had hidden in his clothes and cut himself repeatedly on his chest and arms. Because he sliced numerous veins, his blood began to spurt immediately. In a last effort to absolve himself, he staggered to his feet, dabbed a finger in his blood, and scrawled on the wall, "I am innocent!" Then he fell to the floor and slowly bled to death.

AFTER LORENZO WAS RELEASED from his overnight detention, he drove home and spent so much time in the shower that the hot water ran out. If memories of the bad smells and the bad men of the jail lingered in his mind, at least his body had been cleansed.

He dressed quickly and drove to the office. Now more than ever he knew he had to spend as much time as he could spare on Gus Cortez's case.

"What happened to you?" asked Dolores from the doorway. "You look terrible." She had made coffee and was carrying some sweet rolls she had baked for him.

Lorenzo, his face bruised and his eyes red from lack of sleep, did not answer at first.

"Lorenzo. What is the matter with you?"

"I failed that kid."

"The one with the whore for a sister?"

"Yeah. That's the one."

Dolores handed him a fresh cup of coffee and two rolls on a plate. "Eat these and all will be better."

"Don't I wish," he sighed, as he took a bite of roll and a gulp of coffee.

"I know you did your best," she said, as she walked toward the door. "You always do."

At that moment, the phone rang.

"Lorenzo Madrid."

He listened for a moment, then slumped back in this chair, his face turning pale.

Connie was shouting so loudly at the other end that he had to hold the receiver away from his ear.

"HE OFFED HIMSELF! HE CUT HIMSELF ALL OVER HIS BODY AND HE BLED TO DEATH! YOU FAILED HIM ONCE AGAIN! YOU ARE A TRAITOR TO YOUR PEOPLE!"

◉ ◉ ◉ ◉

That night, Lorenzo went to a bar, something he rarely did. He sat at a small table in the back with another man.

"Another one, please," he said to the waitress, "and for my friend." He turned to Greg Nettles, his longtime friend. "I didn't know what to say to her. I did fail her brother. I didn't try hard enough."

"That's a bunch of bullshit, Lorenzo. I've known you a long time, and I know how hard you fight for your clients. I've met a lot of attorneys in my years on the force and in the DEA, and you've got to be one of the most caring. You take cases no one else will take and for people who have nowhere else to turn. This kid certainly falls into that category, from what you've told me."

"Yeah, his was a hopeless case."

"So why did you agree to help him?"

Lorenzo shrugged and drained his glass. He signaled for another. "If you want to know the truth, I let his sister bully me. She shamed me, yelling about how I let down my people and all that shit. But I do help people in need and most of them are Hispanic. I'm proud of what I've done."

"So why did you let her get to you?"

"I went with her to see Gus in jail, and he looked so pitiful and alone. My heart went out to him. I decided right there that I would help him."

"And you did, so why beat yourself up about this? You need to move on. And you need to have some coffee. You want me to drive you home?"

"No, I'm good. I promise I will eat something and drink black coffee before I go home. I know you need to be on your way. Thanks for listening."

Greg patted Lorenzo on the shoulder. "If you're sure? Good night, buddy. I'll call you tomorrow."

Greg walked out of the bar, but Lorenzo did not order food. He moved to the bar and ordered a glass of beer and a shot of whiskey. After he downed both far too quickly, a blond person walked over to him and sat down.

"Buy a lonely soul a drink?"

The two talked for a few minutes then left the bar together, Lorenzo staggering a bit in the process and the other person asking for the key to his car to drive him home.

◉　◉　◉　◉

The next morning, Lorenzo woke with a start and glanced at the clock on his bedside table. He was lying with only a sheet and a muscular arm stretched across his bare chest.

"God, I can't believe the time!"

The person next to him stirred. "What'd you say, honey?"

"I'm late. I've got to get going!"

A young blond man sat up, the sheet falling away from his well-developed torso. In the days before he met his lover Scott, Lorenzo had cruised the bars of L.A. looking for just a guy like this.

183

"I have to tell you, you were fabulous," he said, reaching over to stroke Lorenzo's back.

"For an old guy, right?" Lorenzo got up and put on a bathrobe.

"No, I mean it. You were great and what a body! But you've got to leave now? Guys usually want more, like a morning-after session," said the young man, feigning sorrow.

"I hate to disappoint you, but I've got things to do. How much do I owe you, John?"

"It's Jim, and I didn't do this for money."

"Look, Jim. Guys like you pick up guys like me for money and maybe some good sex. I can't say I didn't like what we did — what little I remember, that is. But I left that life behind a long time ago. Take some money from my wallet but then please get dressed and leave. I'm going to take a shower."

"I have never been so insulted in my life!" shouted the young man.

"To use the word on everyone's lips today—whatever," replied Lorenzo, as he closed the bathroom door and got in the shower.

After his shower, Lorenzo was relieved to see that Jim had gone. Next to his wallet was a note: "I took $20 for cab fare. I really liked you. Jim." Next to his name he had drawn a heart with an arrow through it.

◉   ◉   ◉   ◉

Late that afternoon, Lorenzo drove to Gates, the small town in the foothills of the Cascade Mountains where the seminary was located. He wasn't sure what he was looking for but decided to look around, given Martindale's tip about the drug operation and Gus's death. To blend in with the largely Hispanic population, he wore a disguise of sorts: a blue work shirt and jeans and a straw hat. He added a thick mustache for good measure, in case anyone from the seminary who would remember him from the trial happened to be around.

The town was hardly that, only one street with a dilapidated convenience store, two bars, and a post office. At the end of the block was a large building with a sign on the window: WORKER COOPERATIVE. He figured that was the place where local men waited each day for someone to hire them for seasonal farm work.

After he walked down one side of the street, he crossed to the other. As he passed one of the bars, three men staggered out.

"What the fuck?" shouted one man to another who had a deep scar on his face. "You let your old mama talk to you like that? What a pussy!"

The man with a scar lunged at the first man and pinned him against the wall. He stepped back and started shouting.

"You want to stay involved in my operation and keep makin' the big bucks by doin' nothin'? Or you want me to cut off your balls and feed them to you for a midnight snack? Don't you EVER talk to me that way again! *Comprende?* Come over here!"

The man complied meekly.

"Stand up straight! Now, speaking of balls, how does this feel?"

Then the scarred man kicked the first man in his groin so hard that he fainted and fell against the wall of the bar. As he fell, Lorenzo had to jump out of the way.

"What're you lookin' at, old man?" said the scarred man.

"*No comprende, señor. No Inglés,*" said Lorenzo.

"Get out of my fuckin' way. Are you deaf as well as dumb?"

Lorenzo pointed to his head and nodded and hurried on. "Dumb wetbacks. They're ruinin' our country!"

Lorenzo guessed that the scarred man had something to do with the drug operation at the seminary—if there was a drug operation at the seminary. As soon as he was a half-mile out of town, Lorenzo parked in a grove of trees, picked up his cell phone, and punched in a number.

"Greg. Lorenzo. I've got something I need to tell you and someone I need you to talk to."

◉　◉　◉　◉

Early the following morning, an unmarked police car drove by a group of hookers on a corner in Portland's Old Town District. The car pulled to the curb, and a man's hand reached out and summoned one of the ladies over to the car. The other women walked away quickly.

Consuelo Cortez hesitated and pointed to herself with a "who me" look on her face. She shrugged and walked over to the car, wobbling as usual in her high heels. She leaned in to talk to Greg Nettles, Lorenzo's friend, who had hitched a ride with a friendly Portland cop.

THE NEXT NIGHT, the full moon slipped behind a cloud and Lorenzo took that moment to run across the yard to a side door at the St. Gregory Seminary. He had observed the building for hours and figured out that this door opened into the library. He watched as lights in various parts of the building went out. Now, at 1 a.m., it seemed like everyone was asleep.

He had come here on a hunch that he might find some kind of records to clear Gus or figure out if people in the seminary—other priests, the housekeeper he had seen in court, whomever—had information that would prove that Gus had not killed Father Gordon. What difference did it make now, with Gus dead? For Lorenzo, it was more than pride. In spite of all her rudeness and bravado, Gus's sister was right: he had failed the young man.

And he was ashamed of himself for not taking the case more seriously. He had allowed himself to be distracted by his own fatigue from doing the job he had sworn an oath to do—be a diligent attorney and friend to those who needed him. He was convinced that inside this old building, high on a hill, he would find the clues he needed to finish this job.

The old lock on the door had been easily jimmied, and the room was dark as he stepped inside. He stopped to listen for any sounds, then turned on his flashlight. The light skittered across the walls that were lined with paintings of men dressed in Catholic vestments. He walked to each painting and pulled on the frames, hoping for one that would swing out and reveal a safe.

The first four yielded nothing, but he got lucky on the fifth one. As he stared into the eyes of a fierce-looking mother superior wearing the starched robes of another time, the frame gave and swung away from the wall. An ancient safe was tucked into a small alcove in the wall.

Holding the flashlight in his teeth, Lorenzo started twirling the dial back and forth, a trick a policeman friend had taught him years ago. He listened for a click and smiled as the old handle yielded and the iron door of the safe swung open so fast that it hit the side of the alcove with a loud bang.

Unsure of what he was looking for, Lorenzo pulled out the first binders he saw and placed them on the large desk in the center of the room. He glanced at his watch. He had been inside this room for seven minutes, half the time he had given himself to try to find the evidence he hoped was here.

He found what he was looking for right away: two binders, one marked "Priest Discipline Records" and the other "Income from RVA." He placed them in the canvas bag he had brought along and quickly put the other binders back in the safe, closed the door as quietly as he could, and put the painting back in position against the wall.

As he was making his way to the door, a light in the hall came on and he heard people whispering. Lorenzo's heart skipped a beat as the door opened and two people walked in, a man and a woman.

"Turn on the lamp, *niño*," said the woman.

"I'm not your *niño*, Ma," said the man. "I'm thirty-five years old!"

"But Paco, your face. That scar. You could have lost an eye."

"Don't touch it, Ma. It's my badge of honor. It makes me look like a real badass, don't you think, Ma?"

"I'd rather have my adorable son in one piece."

"Whatever. Why the fuck are we whispering and creeping around in the dark, for Christ's sake?"

"Do not use the name of the Savior like that in a house of God, Paco!"

"Okay, okay. Turn on the light, Ma. We're safe. It's late and all those queers are upstairs asleep. Maybe not sleeping but ballin' some little kids."

"You should not speak of these men in that way, Paco. They are mostly good and faithful to their vows."

"Oh, I see. Now we have *Señora* Valdez, the loyal housekeeper of this high and mighty seminary. Fuck! What a bunch of crap!"

"Do NOT use such words in my presence! I am your mother and I deserve respect! Your brother would not address me in that manner."

"Oh, yeah. My walk-on-water brother, the priest. How many kids has he molested since his ordination?"

Señora Valdez slapped her son. "Don't you ever say such things about your brother again! On my mother's grave, I will turn you over to the *Federales!*"

Now it was *Señora* Valdez's turn to be hit. Lorenzo peeked out from his hiding place in a closet and saw the woman fall to the floor, holding her face and moaning. Paco walked over to her, rubbing his hand.

"Damn, Ma. I got a pretty good right hook, don't you think? What would I be, a welterweight?"

As he reached down and pulled his mother to her feet, Lorenzo was able to get a good look at him. He was of medium height and weight, with the usual tattoos that most gangbangers adorned their bodies with. The scar his mother had mentioned ran from his right eye to his mouth, giving him an adornment he could use to establish some standing in whatever gang he belonged to. After a minute or two, Lorenzo recognized him as one of the Hispanic men in court during Gus's hearing, and he had also seen him the night before, staggering out of the bar in town.

"I'm sorry, Ma, but you can't say things like that. I love you, but you can't disrespect me like that. What if one of my homies heard you? I'd lose my place as the leader. Worse for you, if *Señor* Robles heard you say that, your ass would be grass. I could not save you from him. He gets real nasty real fast when things don't go his way. You keep your mouth shut about all of this — for both your sake and mine. *Comprende?*"

Señora Robles poured a glass of water and sat down. "What are you looking for, *niño?*"

"That pervert Father Gordon kept records of the money from our drug deals that we sent him to launder."

"I don't understand. Father Gordon washed money for you? How did he keep from ruining it?"

"No, no, Ma," said Paco, chuckling. "We sent him lots of cash, and he ran it through the church accounts to hide it. We gave him a cut, and he used that to keep this place going. Who would suspect a humble priest? Only he wasn't so humble. I also sent him boys, Mexican boys."

Señora Valdez covered her ears and started to cry. "I don't want to hear this!"

"You may not want to hear this, but it's true. *Señor* Robles nearly shit a brick when he heard that Father Gordon was keeping these records. But enough of that shit! I've got to find those binders and take them to *Señor* Robles."

Valdez gave up on his search for the binders quickly, and when he and his mother left the room, Lorenzo was able to slip out the door to the garden.

◉　◉　◉　◉

Lorenzo had dropped the binders off to Greg Nettles early the next day for him to read and make copies of. Now he was meeting with Greg in the same Salem bar as before. Greg slid a bag containing the binders across the table, and Lorenzo put the bag next to him in the booth.

"This stuff is a gold mine, Lorenzo. God, I can't believe you went in there and got these files. Right under their noses." Greg began to recount facts he had read from the files. "Paco Valdez is a nasty little cuss. Lots of arrests since he was twelve years old. At first, just minor stuff, and then he was caught up in a sweep the state police staged a couple of years ago along I-5. That's the main route for drugs into this state, you know."

"So I've heard," said Lorenzo.

"These guys figure to operate in plain sight. No back roads for them. Just mix in with all the regular travelers. We catch a lot of them but a lot also get through. Paco got nabbed and did federal time on McNeal Island. He got out six months ago, and it looks like he didn't learn anything from the experience. His mother is probably nothing more than an enabler for her son. Happy to let her dear baby do whatever he wants to do without knowing much about it."

"What about this guy Robles he kept talking about?" asked Lorenzo.

"Ernesto Robles poses as a businessman and has gotten very rich from his business, whatever it is. He says it's import/export. We don't know for sure, but what he imports is probably cocaine and marijuana. He pays off the Mexican police and some military officers and, as a result, has made himself untouchable. We aren't sure how this latest Oregon connection works, but it sounds like he uses the seminary as a front, with Paco as his local man."

"Can't you close this down?" said Lorenzo. "Can't you lure Robles up here and nab him? You've got these records to expose his operation now, right?"

"That's the problem. We do but we got them—you got them—illegally, without a search warrant. Even though we know what they reveal, a judge wouldn't admit them as evidence. If Robles was even arrested and brought to trial, any high-powered attorney could get us laughed out of court. Even you, Lorenzo, could not change such a ruling."

"So, what do we do?"

"I thought you'd never ask," laughed Greg. "You need to go back to the seminary and put those binders back in that safe. Then we get a friendly judge to give us a warrant so we can go in there and find the records legally."

7

THAT NIGHT, LORENZO WAITED ONCE AGAIN in the shadow
of a big tree near the main building of St. Gregory's. As he had
done a few nights before, he planned to break into the building
and merely place the binders on the desk, then leave. He and
Greg decided that it wasn't really necessary to get the records
back in the safe—that would take extra time that Lorenzo probably wouldn't have. Let Paco wonder how the binders got there.

Lorenzo's thoughts were interrupted by the sound of a car
coming down the driveway. The motor was loud and when the
driver stopped and turned off the ignition, smoke began pouring out from under the hood. The door opened and Lorenzo
could see long, shapely legs emerge. He recognized the shoes
and shook his head.

"No, no!" he muttered. "Not her, not here, not now!"

Consuelo Cortez stood up and straightened her tight dress
and then walked up to the front door in her usual wobbly way.
She rang the bell and when no one answered right away, she
rang it again and again. After five minutes, the door opened and
Señora Valdez stood there, hands on her hips and a defiant look
on her face.

"What do you want? We have no place for your kind here.
This is a house of God."

"What makes you think I'm not a nun in disguise?" Connie
began to laugh at her own joke, but the *señora* was not amused.

"I can tell you right now that you won't be seeing anyone inside this seminary. We do not allow your kind anywhere near these hallowed grounds. Get out of here!"

"I've got business with whoever is in charge of this godforsaken place. My brother killed himself because of one of your good-for-nothing priests!"

Señora Valdez glanced around nervously and then stepped aside to allow Connie to enter the building.

Now Lorenzo had another task. As well as returning the records, he had to get Connie out of there unscathed. He walked quickly around the side of the building to the door of the library, which this time was unlocked.

Lorenzo's thoughts were jumbled because of Connie's unexpected arrival. A lamp was on in the room, and on a whim, he decided to put the binders back in the safe. As he had done before, he moved the painting and began to turn the dial back and forth. While he was listening for the click, the door burst open.

"What the hell do we have here?" said Paco. He entered the room, pushing Connie ahead of him with his mother following close behind.

"That's the lawyer for the kid who killed himself," said *Señora* Valdez. "I remember him from court."

"I'm sorry, Lorenzo," said Connie. "I shouldn't have come here."

"You did kind of foul . . ."

Paco walked over to Lorenzo. "Shut up, pretty boy!" He began to run his hand over Lorenzo's face. "You are too pretty to be a man. Are you sure you are a man?"

"I was the last time I looked."

"Paco, please," said *Señora* Valdez. "Do not disgrace me."

"Shut up, Ma! What I don't understand, *Señor* Lorenzo, is why you came here. You know we could call the cops and get you arrested for breakin' and enterin'. Ha, ha, ha. But I guess we won't be doin' that, now will we? Why did you come here? Lookin' for your girlfriend? A whore like her? You can do much better than that. Like maybe even with me. Ha, ha, ha, ha." Then he saw the binders on the floor by the safe and walked over to pick them up. "Son of a bitch! You read this stuff, you read all about our little venture here? *Madre mia!* I am fucked if *Señor* Robles finds that out. Oh god, oh god. I'll be lucky if he doesn't feed me to the sharks or turn me over to his Mexican goons!"

"Paco, you've got to get them out of here because if anyone sees them, I don't want . . ."

"Ma, I told you to shut the fuck up! I've got to think."

"Now, that would be a novel reaction," said Connie with a smirk. "Guys like you never think beyond the bulge in their pants."

Paco raised his hand to hit Connie, but Lorenzo lunged for him and they both fell to the floor, Paco on top. He hit Lorenzo several times in the face and then got up and kicked him in the groin. Lorenzo groaned and rolled over in a fetal position.

"Damn, I'm good," said Paco, rubbing his hands. "I hate to ruin that beautiful face of yours and those magnificent balls you no doubt have, but you shouldn't have jumped me like that. And, worst of all, you shouldn't have looked at those records. God, I can't save your pretty ass for myself if *Señor* Robles finds out. I'm only tryin' to protect what's mine."

"Yours!" screamed Connie. "You think you own me? Not in this lifetime, *amigo!*"

"Unfortunately for you, baby, you are in this thing up to your hoop earrings. You may have been tryin' to avenge your baby brother, but you stumbled into something that may not have an outcome you'll like. The guy I work for, *Señor* Robles, does not like outsiders stickin' their noses into his affairs. If you're lucky, he won't have you killed. He'll probably just send you out of the country. But who would miss a two-bit whore like you? Come on, little lady, let me look at you again."

Paco moved Connie into the light and shoved her into a chair. "Not bad for an older chick with some wear and tear on her. I'd lose the red hair and maybe a few pounds. Not bad otherwise. He'll probably sell you to his Asian friends, and you'll wind up someplace exotic. You'll get some nice clothes out of it and, if you're lucky, you won't get the clap or AIDS."

"In your dreams, punk! I don't intend to go anywhere with . . ."

At that point, Paco plunged a needle into Connie's arm, and she fell out of the chair onto the floor.

As Lorenzo began to stir, Paco walked over to him. "A true sleeping beauty," he said, pulling Lorenzo up by the shoulders and leaning him against the sofa. Then he stuck the same needle into Lorenzo's arm, who fell over sideways.

WHEN HE FIRST WOKE UP, Lorenzo wasn't sure where he was, but then it began to come back to him. He and Connie had been discovered at the seminary by Paco, but he wasn't sure what had happened next.

He sensed motion so he knew he was in some kind of vehicle—probably a truck. It was too dark to tell for sure, but he smelled onions. He tried to move but soon realized that his hands were tied behind him and his feet were shackled. He felt something in the corner of his mouth: congealed blood.

A brief flash of light illuminated the area, allowing him to see a wall of crates placed to allow an area only big enough for him.

"God, where am I? I feel like shit."

. . . and Connie.

"Connie."

"What? Who is it?"

"Lorenzo. You remember me, the guy who ruined your life."

"You got THAT right, *amigo!*"

"We're in the back of a truck. I'd guess a produce truck. Smell the onions?"

"God, I hate onions!"

"I think they're taking us to Mexico."

"Mexico? Am I dreaming? I left that place a long time ago, and I sure as hell don't want to go back. How did you get here?"

"You remember the seminary? You went there, and I broke in."

"To save me? Maybe Gus was right about you after all."

"I didn't actually go there to save you. I was putting back some files about what's been going on at the seminary."

"You mean the drug deals and money laundering? Your friend Greg told me all about it. After that, all I could think of was to go there and see if I could find out something to clear Gus's name. I guess I screwed up, didn't I?"

"It does complicate things to have you involved. I was prepared to do what I had to do to figure out who killed Father Gordon, but now . . ."

"Now you've got to deal with me. I'm sorry. We're going to die, just like Gus. We know too much, like he must have." She sniffled a few times. "Hell, I can't even wipe my nose. Who's got us, anyway?"

"You remember that guy named Paco?"

"Oh, yeah. A real creep."

"He's the one who drugged us and kidnapped us. He works for a man named Robles, who must be a cartel boss. I think Paco screwed up by being careless with the records I found and also by taking us wherever we're going. A guy like Robles does not like loose ends, and we are definitely that."

Just then the truck stopped abruptly, the crates were pushed aside, and Paco stuck his head in.

"So, the two of you are back with us," he said. "Getting acquainted? We're going to let you out a minute to pee. I am a real benevolent SOB, don't you think? Ha, ha, ha, ha! Chito, get your tight little ass in here!"

A young Hispanic man stepped around Paco and walked over to Connie to untie her hands and feet. He helped her up and led her out of the truck. Then he went back for Lorenzo,

198

unlocking the leg restraints and cutting off the plastic ties around his wrists.

Lorenzo rubbed his wrists and ankles. "Nice to get some blood circulating again."

Chito pulled Lorenzo to his feet, but Lorenzo was dizzy and he staggered a bit until Chito steadied him.

"Now, isn't that a touching scene," sneered Paco. "Two queers dancing. Get him out of there! Now!"

When Lorenzo's feet touched the ground, someone put a hood over his head and led him away from the truck. The terrain was rough, and he stumbled a few times. Then they stopped and the hood was pulled off.

"Go over there behind those trees, if you want," said Chito.

After Lorenzo had finished, Chito replaced the hood and led him back to the truck.

Soon he heard Connie's voice. "Get your hands off me, you creep!"

"Okay, okay," said Paco, laughing. "I like my women wild. I think I'll call you Wildcat when I introduce you to *Señor* Robles. Or maybe Hot Tamale. Now shut the fuck up! Put 'em back in the truck, Chito. We need to get movin'. To the land of my birth, Mexico. Old Mexico, how I miss it so. If I had a guitar, I would sing something for you."

"If you had a guitar," hissed Connie, "I'd hit you over the head with it."

Paco turned to Connie and slapped her across the face. "I can't stand women who disrespect me. Did that sting a little?" He put two fingers close together to measure the sting. "Ha, ha, ha, ha! It'll only hurt for a little bit but maybe, just maybe it will teach you to show me some respect."

"In your dreams will I ever respect you!" shouted Connie.

"Maybe we should give them some food and water, Paco," said Chito, trying to break the tension. "They won't be any good to you if they're weak from not eating. And they're probably dehydrated."

"Now, you're a compassionate little guy, aren't you?" said Paco. "Shit, I suppose you're right. Okay, give 'em some food and water."

As Chito helped them up into the truck, Lorenzo whispered to him, "You need to help us get away. You're not like Paco, I can see that. I know all of this bothers you."

Chito pulled away and glanced nervously at Paco, who had turned and walked away. "I'll be back."

He returned soon with two bottles of water and plates of food, which he handed to Connie and Lorenzo. He motioned for them to move to the back of the truck.

"*Frijoles* and *tortillas*," said Connie. "Tastes good." She ate quickly and took several gulps of water.

"Help us, please," said Lorenzo, when he had finished eating.

At that point, Paco pushed the crates aside and stuck his head in. "What's takin' so long?"

"They just finished eating," said Chito, collecting their plates but leaving the water bottles.

"Make it fast, little *amigo*. We've got to get out of here. We've got to make up some time 'cuz we've got someone *muy importante* to meet."

Paco walked away, and Chito leaned down to put the shackles on Lorenzo's ankles.

"What happened when you went to Father Gordon's cottage that night?" asked Lorenzo.

Chito looked startled. "How'd you know about that?"

"Someone saw you with him and told me. I saw you in court too. No time to explain now."

"That kid on the path to the cottage. Was that Gus?"

"What the fuck is going on here?" yelled Paco. "Are you havin' a meeting without me? Ha, ha, ha, ha."

"I'm just tying them up," said Chito.

"That better be all you're doin'. Get the fuck out of there. I've got a little present for our guests."

Paco grabbed Lorenzo's arm and inserted a needle so quickly that he could not pull away. Connie screamed as he did the same thing to her. As they both passed out, all Lorenzo heard was Paco's hideous laugh. "Ha, ha, ha, ha, ha!"

LORENZO COULD TELL that he was in more comfortable surroundings when he woke up. No more hard truck bed, no more crates, no more onion smell. He was in some kind of storeroom with dim rays of sun coming through closed blinds. There were also chairs and tables and a lot of boxes pushed up against one another.

"Where are we?"

Lorenzo turned toward Connie's voice. It took a few seconds for him to find her—she had slipped behind some of the boxes.

"In a house, a pretty nice house, I'd guess near the U.S./ Mexico border. It's hot enough to be in the desert, but it doesn't seem like we were passed out long enough to have driven the length of California."

"My head hurts," she moaned. "I feel like I've been drinking all day and all night. You may not believe this, but I don't drink. At least, not anymore. I'm reformed. I know you think of me as a two-bit whore—I can't help that. I am what I am, and I do what I have to do to survive."

"Look, Connie, we've got more to worry about than my opinion of you," said Lorenzo, straining against his leg irons. "For the record, though, I think you've had to make choices in your life like we all do, and you did what you did to save Gus. Let's just leave it at that. We need to concentrate on getting out of here." Lorenzo tried to move his legs and arms but nothing would budge. "I'm cinched up so tight I can't move."

"Where'd you say we are?"

"They want us to think we're in Mexico but I'm not sure. If we are there, we're probably just over the border, maybe near Tijuana, but that's just a guess."

Connie sighed. "Can you believe that I once tried to work as a prostitute in Tijuana? When I was still a teenager. I was so fucked up then that I thought I could make lots of money and take care of my family. Shit, what else could I do? I was only in school through the second grade. But, I had the looks then. I had great boobs, even as a kid. I even fantasized that I could buy my family a house. That hope lasted only one night after my pimp took most of the money I earned. Then he beat me up and asked why I hadn't earned more. I walked back over the border the next day."

The door opened, letting in more sunlight and illuminating the room. Paco was standing in the doorway, a smirk on his face.

"Now that is what I call a touching story. Poor little Consuelo. Even her big teenage boobies couldn't get her out of the cess-pool she was born into. Ha, ha, ha, ha. Chito, untie them so they can pee and eat some food."

Chito walked into the room quickly and untied Connie's hands and unlocked her leg restraints. Then he did the same for Lorenzo. He helped them to their feet, and the three turned toward the doorway.

Paco stood there with his arms crossed and his feet wide apart, as if surveying some possessions. "Okay, there's a bath-room at the end of the hall," he said. "You first, Consuelo." He pushed her ahead of him down the hall, and Lorenzo and Chito followed. "Ain't I nice? I believe in that Gentlemen's Convention for treating prisoners of war. You know, all those important dudes got together after some bullshit war and held a convention in a big hall overseas in Europe or Africa or some-place like that."

"It's called the Geneva Convention," said Lorenzo.

Paco walked over to Lorenzo and got close to his face. "You callin' me a liar, Mr. Pretty Boy Lawyer?"

Lorenzo squelched a smile. "I would never do that, Paco. I just thought you'd want to use the correct name. Easy to make a mistake about stuff like that. All I wanted to do was be helpful."

Paco's eyes flashed. "You won't be so high and mighty when *Señor* Robles gets here with his guys. I ain't got enough men to do this job properly."

Paco walked away, leaving Chito in charge. Chito opened the bathroom door, and Connie went inside.

"What's going to happen here?" asked Lorenzo. "And where are we? Mexico?"

"Not yet," Chito replied. "We're in a remote part of southeastern Oregon. I'm not sure how *Señor* Robles found this place, but he's built a nice house here, like a Mexican hacienda. There's desert all around us. And an airstrip. I think it's a place where he comes to rest, but there's also a big warehouse for packing up the drugs for shipment."

"Hide in plain sight," said Lorenzo.

"What do you mean?"

"I mean that he does all of this on U.S. soil in a place he thinks is beyond the reach of the cops."

At that moment, both Lorenzo and Chito looked up as they heard the distant whine of a jet engine powering down.

"Sounds like the man is here," said Chito. "Things could get a lot worse pretty fast. Robles is a sadist—loves to hurt people even more than Paco does." He walked to the bathroom door. "*Señorita*, you must hurry."

The door opened and Connie stepped out. She had combed her hair and washed her face. "Your turn," she said to Lorenzo.

Lorenzo walked into the bathroom and closed the door.

"You must hurry," Chito yelled after him. "Paco will be anxious to show off his captives."

Five minutes later, Paco came stomping down the hall. "What the fuck is all this delay? Where's pretty boy?"

Chito pointed to the bathroom.

Paco walked to the door and flung it open. "Catch you with your pants down?" he asked, laughing.

"Not your lucky day," said Lorenzo, who was drying his face on a dirty towel.

"Come on, come on. You're pretty enough," shouted Paco. He grabbed both Lorenzo and Connie by their arms and pushed them down the hall into a large room with expensive-looking leather sofas in front of a very large flat-screen TV. "Sit, sit, sit!"

As they obeyed him, a door to the outside opened and an older, well-dressed man entered, followed by two younger men with shaved heads covered with tattoos. Both carried assault rifles and showed no emotion on their faces.

The older man walked over to Connie. "Please stand up, *señorita*, so I can get a good look at you."

Connie obliged.

"You'll do for now because I'm kind of horny. I must say, you are kind of old to be in this line of work. But as that great American president Benjamin Franklin once said, 'In the dark, they are all the same'."

"Who, *patrón?*" asked Paco.

"Benjamin Franklin, the father of this country, you moron. Don't you know anything about your adopted country? He freed the slaves and settled the war with Mexico."

Paco shrugged. "Sorry, *Señor* Robles. I must have been absent from school that day." He gestured toward Connie. "Do you want me to keep her around or sell her to our Asian friends right away?"

"I'm not givin' any of what I've got to you for free!" shouted Connie, defiantly. "That's for sure."

Robles just smiled at her.

"Do you realize that trafficking in human beings across state lines is a federal offense in the United States?" said Lorenzo. "I take it we are still in the United States, so that means you are subject to federal penalties, and they're pretty severe. Add to that your drug ring, and I'd say you are looking at many years behind bars, *Señor* Robles."

Robles turned to his men. "I'll give this *hombre* one thing, he's got balls. Right *amigos*?"

At his signal, the two of them and Paco started laughing.

Robles moved close to Lorenzo and said, "So, we've got ourselves an attorney here. An attorney with all the answers. Keep your mouth shut, or I will have my friends here make sure you don't have a mouth or a tongue to ever talk again. *Comprende?*"

"Look, Robles, I'm not interested in your drug operation. I only got into this to clear Connie's brother. He was being railroaded into prison for a crime he did not do."

"Tell it to the judge," said Robles. "Ha, ha, ha, ha. Not too bad a joke. But I've got my own attorneys. I don't need some pretty boy telling me about the law. I am the law!"

"That's tellin' 'em, boss," shouted Paco.

"Shut up, Paco," snarled Robles. "You screwed up once again. Why'd you bring these people here? Now they know where we are and what we're doing."

Paco sputtered, "I . . . figured . . . you'd want me . . ."

"You know what, Paco," said Robles, "you are too dumb to figure out anything of importance." He turned to the two goons and rubbed his head. "Get 'em back to the storeroom. I've got to think."

The two gang members pushed Lorenzo and Connie back into the hall and down to the storeroom. They ignored Paco, who looked miserable. Chito followed at a distance and slipped inside as the door closed.

"Here's some water," said Chito. "Not sure I can find any food right now."

"Thanks, Chito," said Lorenzo. "I'm glad you're helping us, but you're taking a big chance, as you must know. Robles wouldn't think twice about letting those two goons break your neck."

"It's like you said before—I can kind of hide in plain sight," he said. "I just try to blend in, and people seem to ignore me as a harmless kid. So I figure, what do I have to lose?"

"How'd you get hooked up with Paco in the first place?"

"He's a psychopath, but he can be charming. When I was fifteen, he talked my mother into letting him adopt me. Nothing official, but that's what he told her. She agreed to let him, she said for my sake—with ten other kids, I guess she had no choice."

"Poor kid," said Consuelo.

"He and I crossed the border together, just like in the movies, swimming across the Rio Grande with our stuff rolled up in

207

plastic bags. I guess I should be grateful to him for getting me into this country and what I thought would be a better life."

"But I gather that isn't what happened," said Lorenzo.

"No. Far from it," said Chito, shaking his head with a sad look on his face. "Pretty soon, I found out that all he wanted was a young piece of ass to supplement all his girlfriends. He's a sex addict, no question."

"Just like what happened to Gus," said Connie.

"Did Paco use you as bait with Father Gordon?" asked Lorenzo.

"Yeah, I'm afraid so," said Chito, hanging his head. "Once he found out that the priest liked young boys, I became *numero uno*."

"You poor kid," Connie said again.

"You've got to help us get out of here," said Lorenzo. "Is there a back door to this place?"

"Sure, through the garage," said Chito, walking over to the door and glancing out. "Doesn't look like anyone's there now."

"Okay, then, here's what we're going to do," said Lorenzo. "Sorry, but I'm going to have to knock you out."

10

THE LIGHT FROM A SMALL FLASHLIGHT illuminated the walls of the cave Lorenzo and Connie were in.

"God, it's so cold," she said. "Can't you start a fire?"

"With what? Two flashlights rubbed together?"

The sad look on her face indicated that even Connie was not oblivious to hurt feelings.

"Sorry, Connie. I didn't mean to be snotty. I know you're cold and tired and hungry. Drink some water and eat this apple. It's the last thing we've got to eat."

They had made an easy exit from the hacienda—Lorenzo supposed everyone was having a siesta, even the guards. The terrain near the ranch was flat, and they walked for two hours before arriving at a small escarpment on the edge of the desert. In its face was the cave where they were now resting.

"It'll be better to travel at night," he said. "It'll be colder, but the bad guys won't be able to find us as easily."

Connie sighed. "I guess they won't stop looking for us."

"Not a chance," said Lorenzo. "We know too much about Robles. Frankly, I'm surprised he didn't kill us already."

Connie started to cry. In seconds, her whole body was shaking from her heavy sobs.

"That doesn't mean we have to sit back and take it," Lorenzo said, patting her hand. "Now, let's get some sleep. I'll wake you when it's safe to go."

After three hours, he did just that.

"Rise and shine, Connie. Time to hit the road."

Connie moaned and turned over to face him. "I was dreaming of having sex with a tall, dark, and handsome stranger. He was Hispanic and he looked a lot like you."

"I'm sure you say that to all the guys," said Lorenzo. "No time for any hanky panky now."

"What's hanky panky?" she asked.

"Never mind. Get up and get ready. It's after midnight, and we've got to make some time before morning. I'm hoping we find a house with a telephone." He looked at her feet, which were swollen and bleeding and said, "Give me your shoes."

"No. I can't walk without shoes, Lorenzo."

"Just trust me. Hand 'em over."

She did so reluctantly. He broke off the high heels and handed the shoes back to her.

"It'll make it easier to walk, at least I hope so."

She put them on and stood up, then gave him a thumbs-up sign. Lorenzo helped Connie down from the ledge, and they set out in what Lorenzo hoped was a northerly direction. After a half-hour, the ground turned into deep sand, which made it very hard to walk. Each step took longer, slowing them down.

After another hour, Connie stopped and sat down. "I'm pooped. I can't go on. I don't think I can make it."

Lorenzo took her hand and started pulling her along through the sand, like a pack horse pulling a travois. After fifteen minutes, he stopped and dropped down beside her.

"I guess I'm more out of shape than I thought I was."

"I'm cold and miserable," she moaned. "I never thought I'd miss the mean streets of Portland."

Lorenzo unbuttoned his shirt and took it off. "Here, put this on. It's only cotton, but it might warm you up a little." He stood and walked up a nearby rise in the ground. "Looks like some dim lights a half-mile or so ahead."

Lorenzo helped Connie get to her feet, and they walked on for a little while.

Suddenly, she fell over a downed tree and landed on her face. As she rolled over and started to sit up, she saw a long, dark form near her. "What's that?" she asked Lorenzo.

"Don't move!" shouted Lorenzo, shining his flashlight in her direction. A large rattlesnake was moving slowly toward Connie. "It's cold like we are," said Lorenzo, "and it's attracted to your body heat. Stay calm and don't move."

"Please help me! God, what a way to die! Out in the middle of nowhere. What did I do to deserve this?!"

Lorenzo moved in quickly, grabbed the snake by its tail, and flung it as far away as he could.

"Heavy critter. I now have a new skill beyond my legal expertise: snake-thrower."

Connie started sobbing loudly. "How can you make jokes at a time like this? I could have died."

"But you didn't. You survived. Let's keep moving."

They continued walking, but after a while Connie fell to her knees. "I've had it. I can't go another step."

"Just a little farther and . . ."

He stopped talking when they both heard the whirring sound of a helicopter in the distance.

"Somebody's looking for us," said Lorenzo. "Thank God. Maybe my friend Greg with the DEA or some other government agency. Hell, I don't know. Somebody. Helicopters are not that common out here."

They kept looking in the direction of the sound. In a few minutes, they could see the flashing lights as the aircraft began to descend. When light flashed along the craft, Lorenzo caught a glimpse of an emblem on the side. It did not represent any official government agency. Instead, he saw a skull and the word ROBLES emblazoned on the side.

"Run, Connie! Run as fast as you can! It's Robles and his goons!"

They both started running away from where the helicopter was headed and the men who were shimmying down ropes toward the ground. They ran several hundred yards before they hit a stretch of ground that was as soft as quicksand—and began to sink.

"I'm sinking!" shouted Connie. "I'm going to die—again!"

Lorenzo reached for her and barely managed to grab her hand. Then he began to sink too. "Hold tight," he said, "and don't struggle!"

Even though they tried to remain calm, they kept sinking lower and lower. Just then, powerful hands placed straps around them, and they started rising in the air as the helicopter pulled them to safety. Within minutes, both Lorenzo and Connie were lying on the floor of the helicopter, gasping for breath. Lorenzo looked to one side and saw the silver-tipped toes of boots next to his face. Someone rolled him over on his back, and the man with the boots started kicking him all over. He curled up into a ball and tried to protect his face.

"How did you think you could get away from me, *señor*? You are one stupid bastard."

FIVE PEOPLE WITH HOODS OVER THEIR HEADS were on their knees. *Señor* Robles, a revolver in one hand, walked along in front of them. He pulled the hood off the first one, a young Hispanic man, and shot him between the eyes. He did the same with the second man.

Lorenzo caught a glimpse of the men through a hole in his hood. At first, Lorenzo did not think he had seen them before. Then he remembered them as the men who were with Paco the first time he saw him coming out of the bar in Gates. Two disposable gangbangers.

When he was standing in front of the last three, Robles pulled the hoods off all of them. He looked at Chito, who was shaking uncontrollably.

"You little pissant," hissed Robles. "Take this like a man." Robles raised his pistol, cocked it, and held it next to Chito's forehead. The young man's face was covered with bruises and one eye was swollen shut. His pants were torn and he was shirtless, with cuts visible on his stomach. Chito continued to shake and then pissed his pants, the urine running down his legs and puddling on the ground.

The sight amused Robles. "Ha, ha, ha, ha. A shame to see such a lovely-looking boy so banged up. What happened to you, *amigo?* Ha, ha, ha, ha. I love to see my enemies quake with fear. I love that feeling of power. You like that feeling too, eh Paco?"

"*Si, patrón.*"

Next, Robles stepped in front of Connie, whose face was contorted in fear, her once carefully made-up face now a mask of smeared mascara and red, blotchy skin. He fired his still-cocked pistol into the air. Connie screamed and passed out, her body crumpling to the ground.

Then Robles turned to Lorenzo. "I did not kill her, *Señor* Madrid. She was just very fearful, as you should be as well. I am like Mother Nature. You do not dare mess with me! Ha, ha, ha, ha." He moved to stand in front of Lorenzo, who had a black eye and bruises on his face, and cupped Lorenzo's chin in one hand.

"Get it over with, Robles," said Lorenzo. "I know how much you love to kill people. Does it give you sexual gratification to do this?"

Robles slapped Lorenzo so hard his teeth rattled. "All in good time, *señor*, but I had such wonderful plans for all of you," he said. "The *señorita* would have been the star of my harem. You could have been my lawyer in the United States. I would pay you more money than you could dream about." He gazed into space as if contemplating what might have been.

"I don't believe you for a moment, Robles," said Lorenzo. "Why are you saying these things? And to an audience of one— me. I can't figure . . ."

Robles held up his hand. "*Bastante!* In my business, you always need smart people to guide you. I thought you might be that person, once I brought you around to my point of view." He sighed. "Unfortunately, you chose another path and tried to get away from me. I do not like people who do not see things my way. In my country, we have a way of dealing with people like you. If we cut off your finger, it means you ratted on us. If we remove your tongue, it means you said something to the wrong people. If we cut off a hand, it means we caught you stealing. If we cut off your legs, it means you left our organization and joined a rival one."

Robles shook his head and walked away, saying over his shoulder, "I have not decided exactly what you have done, *Señor* Big-Shot Attorney. Maybe all of these things. I will have to think about your punishment. In the meantime, I'll let you kneel there in the hot sun for a while. Maybe its rays will clear your thoughts."

Lorenzo did not reply. In fact, his throat was suddenly so dry, he doubted that any words would escape his lips, even if he tried to speak.

Robles's men followed him back into the hacienda. Lorenzo, Connie, and Chito were left where the cool of the morning had long since been replaced by the scorching sun. They were soon sweating, their lips dry and bleeding from lack of water.

When the sun was high in the sky, Lorenzo opened his eyes at the sound of a big truck pulling up to the large warehouse near the house. Workers began to haul bales of what was probably cocaine on dollies up a ramp and into the trailer.

After what seemed like many hours, Robles and Paco and the other men walked out of the front door of the hacienda. All were strutting and smoking cigars. In deference to his boss, Paco was walking a few steps behind. Robles walked up to Lorenzo, a lighted cigar in his hand.

"Have you ever smoked a good Cuban cigar, *señor?*"

"No, I have not," said Lorenzo, clearing his throat and straining to find his voice.

"Ever been branded by one?"

Robles suddenly rammed the cigar into Lorenzo's neck, causing him to wince in pain, but he did not cry out.

"I love the smell of flesh burning in the afternoon, don't you, *mi compañeros?*"

The men laughed uproariously.

"So, how are we all on this fine afternoon? Does it pain you to see some of your own people go so bad?"

Lorenzo looked directly at Robles, his eyes flashing. "Most of MY people, as you call them, are not bad. They work hard and try to stay away from people like you."

Paco ran over to Lorenzo and hit him in the mouth. "Do not disrespect *mi patrón* in that manner! He is our leader and an inspiration to us all."

Now it was Lorenzo's turn to laugh. "If that is who you use for an inspiration, it's no wonder you turned out to be such a worthless shit." Then he spit out the blood which had started pooling in his mouth.

Paco started to hit Lorenzo again, but Robles fired his gun into the air. "Enough! You have a tendency to take everything too far, Paco. You are like an unguided missile. I can never trust you to do the right thing. Ever!" Saying that, Robles aimed his gun at Paco's chest and pulled the trigger. The astonished look on Paco's face lasted only seconds before he fell to the ground.

"I should have done that years ago," said Robles. "That man caused me nothing but trouble from the moment I hired him." He turned to the other men. "Get him out of my sight. When I am finished with these three, we'll load them all in the plane and throw them out somewhere over Mexico."

Both Connie and Chito were sobbing loudly at this point.

"Let them go, Robles," said Lorenzo. "They are innocent. I'm the one who caused you all the trouble. They'll be so scared of you, I'm sure they'll keep quiet. I'll be your attorney like you want. I specialize in hopeless causes. I'll keep you out of jail. If I don't do what you want, or if they try to turn you in, you can kill me."

Robles smiled. "I do not consider myself a hopeless case, señor. I am a leader of men. I am a man of substance. I am respected in my country. Let them go and hire you? After all the trouble you have caused me?" He turned to the other men. "Isn't that the biggest joke you have ever heard, *amigos?*"

As if on cue, the men started laughing again, that false kind of laugh where what is being said may not be that funny but you think you'd better laugh anyway.

"Enough of this delay!" shouted Robles. "Pick her up and take her inside!" He pointed at Connie, and one of the men started toward her.

Lorenzo, who had realized that the plastic zip-tie was loose enough to work it off his hands, lunged at Robles and grabbed him by the neck. "One of the things I learned in my years in the barrio is how to kill someone by crushing his windpipe. You may doubt me, *señor*, but do you want to take the chance?" he said, as he tightened his grip on Robles's throat.

Then he shouted to Connie and Chito. "Move over here behind me and untie each other!" The two quickly obeyed him. "Chito, take the gun and hold it next to his head. If I tell you to do so, I want you to pull the trigger."

Lorenzo turned to the gangbangers. "You *hombres* throw down your weapons and get down on your knees."

"Do as he says or he'll kill me," said Robles in a raspy voice.

The men did as he ordered.

Chito held the gun to Robles's head, but his hands were shaking.

"Steady, Chito. Hold the gun steady," Lorenzo said as he secured the plastic strips around Robles's hands.

"How do you expect this boy with no *cajones* to handle me or my men?" taunted Robles.

"Give me the gun, Chito."

"My men will eat him for breakfast as soon as he gets near them," continued Robles.

Lorenzo took the gun from Chito and hit Robles in the face with it. Robles cried out in pain and fell to the ground.

"Shut up, Robles. You're not in charge anymore." He turned to Connie. "See if you can find some rope inside the barn." Then he yelled to the men who had been loading the truck. "You guys take off. I have no quarrel with you."

The men ran to a dilapidated pickup and drove off in a cloud of dust.

Connie returned with several lengths of rope and a roll of strapping tape.

"Wrap the tape around those men as tight as you can," Lorenzo said to Connie.

Connie started circling the men with the tape, after tying their hands behind them with the rope.

"Aren't you the high and mighty hero all of a sudden," said a voice behind them. "What about me? I guess you forgot about me. I have returned from the dead," said Paco, a knife in his hand.

"Paco, thank God, my son," said Robles, his face in the dirt. "Help me, and we'll take care of these people together."

"What a load of bullshit that is," hissed Paco. "If I was your 'son', as you put it, why did you shoot me? Luckily, I bought myself a bulletproof vest a long time ago. I respected you, *patrón*, but I did not trust you. You underestimated me—I'm not quite as dumb as you think I am. Now, Mr. Fancy Lawyer, throw the gun to me."

Lorenzo threw the gun toward Paco.

Paco picked up the gun and said, "Good. It feels good to be in charge of my new organization."

"Your organization!" said Robles, virtually spitting out his words. "That is a big laugh! The other bosses in the cartel would never allow an idiot like you to take anything over, especially a business this important. They will laugh at you and send you on your way—if they don't kill you first! Ha, ha, ha, ha. That is the best laugh I have had in many years. You, the leader of my . . ."

At that moment, Paco walked over to Robles and shot him in the back of his head. His body heaved once, then was still, with blood from his nose and mouth seeping out onto the ground. Then Paco moved toward Lorenzo, throwing the gun to the side.

"I don't need no gun to finish you off, pretty boy! I will use my hunting knife so I can cut your pretty face before I stab you in the heart."

Paco and Lorenzo started a kind of dance around one another, with Paco thrusting his knife at Lorenzo and Lorenzo dodging and moving away each time. In one desperate move, Paco managed to nick Lorenzo's hand. Soon, however, Paco was winded.

"You're not in such good shape, Paco," said Lorenzo, chuckling. "Too many drugged-out nights, too much time with all those whores."

"Shut the fuck up! I can beat an old man like you any day!" He lunged at Lorenzo again but lost his balance and fell on his back. He looked up at Lorenzo, his eyes flashing. "Do it! Do it! I'm tired of fighting!"

"Kill him! Kill him!" yelled Connie and Chito.

Suddenly, the roar of truck engines and bright lights filled the area, and someone started yelling through a loudspeaker: "THIS IS THE DRUG ENFORCEMENT ADMINISTRATION! LAY DOWN YOUR WEAPONS AND PUT YOUR HANDS WHERE WE CAN SEE THEM!"

A WEEK LATER, Lorenzo, Connie, and Chito stepped out of a car and started walking down a hill toward a grave.

"How did the feds track us?" asked Chito.

"My friend Greg is with the DEA, and I had told him what I was doing in a sketchy way," said Lorenzo. "I didn't tell him too much because I knew he'd try to stop me. He said that the DEA had been tracking Robles and his gang for several months but hadn't made the connection to the seminary and the dead priest until I showed him the records I found. Without a proper search warrant, the records could not be introduced in court as evidence. He asked me to put the records back, then get out of there fast. Of course, we know what happened to that plan."

"Tracking, as in following us all along?" asked Connie, her eyes flashing. "Nice of them to let us get in all this danger, then save us just before it was too late! I think I'll sue them up the kazoo. Will you take my case, Lorenzo?"

Both Lorenzo and Chito looked at her quizzically, then all three burst into laughter.

Their faces turned somber as they reached the open grave. Connie lifted the urn she was carrying and leaned over to place it in the space provided. Lorenzo threw a red rose in on top of it. The three then bowed their heads.

"May Gustavo Cortez rest in peace," said Lorenzo.

Connie and Chito crossed themselves, and they all turned around to walk back up the hill.

"Wait!" said Chito. "I've got something to tell you. I killed Father Gordon. He was making me crazy with all his demands for sex. He wouldn't leave me alone. Paco made me do it and threatened to kill me if I tried to stop. He used me to blackmail the priest into letting him run the drug money through the seminary's records."

He turned to Connie, tears in his eyes. "The night your brother saw me, I'd had enough. I put a pillow over the priest's face while he was sleeping and then ran. I didn't know your brother would be blamed, I really didn't."

Connie walked over to him and put her arms around him. Then she began rocking him back and forth. "It's okay, *niño.* It's okay."

"I'll drive you to the police station, Chito," said Lorenzo. "And I'll take your case, of course. I can think of a half-dozen defenses to use when we go to trial. Under these circumstances, maybe there won't need to be a trial. The judge and the police and the D.A. look bad over what happened to Gus. And I won't let them forget it."

The three of them continued walking up the hill toward the car, Lorenzo lagging slightly behind. Several hundred yards off to the left, Lorenzo noticed something that caused him to stop.

Although he would never tell anyone about what he is certain happened, the specter of Gus Cortez appeared briefly and he was smiling.

"He is innocent," muttered Lorenzo, as he resumed his walk to the car.